"If I can figure out a way to free up some of your time, will you promise to spend a day with me?"

"Sure, and buy me a winning lottery ticket while you're at it," Jodie replied.

Jeff ignored her sarcasm and went back to her initial agreement. "You promise? One full day?"

"My first free day is at least four years away, if you can wait that long—"

"I'm betting within the next two weeks," he said. And he was serious.

She shook her head in disbelief. "Not unless you're a miracle worker."

"I'm a marine. We're trained to do the impossible. I'll fulfill my end of the bargain. Be prepared to keep yours."

Okay, so he'd pledged Jodie the impossible, and he hadn't a clue how he'd deliver on that promise.

But as he'd said, he was a marine. He'd think of something—anything—to spend some time alone with her.

Dear Reader,

In the words of an ancient Chinese saying, we live in interesting times. Due to tumultuous world events, we appreciate more than ever security, solace, acceptance and love as bulwarks against the troubles of the day. In my series A PLACE TO CALL HOME I've created a small town in upstate South Carolina where love and acceptance, along with only the occasional mayhem, abound. For the residents of Pleasant Valley, friends are family, and family is everything.

In *One Good Man*, book two of the series, Jeff Davidson, the town's resident bad boy, returns home after serving with the marines. Military service has turned his life around, and he hopes to do the same for delinquent teenage boys by converting his farm into a rehabilitation center. But Jodie Nathan, a single mother with a hell-on-wheels fourteen-year-old daughter, finds Jeff's plans her worst nightmare—and Jeff the man of her dreams.

I hope you'll enjoy watching the sparks fly in Jeff and Jodie's story, and, as we say in the South, y'all come back and visit Pleasant Valley again in book three, *Spring in the Valley*, in April.

Happy reading!

Charlotte Douglas

ONE GOOD MAN
Charlotte Douglas

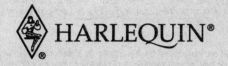

HARLEQUIN®

TORONTO • NEW YORK • LONDON
AMSTERDAM • PARIS • SYDNEY • HAMBURG
STOCKHOLM • ATHENS • TOKYO • MILAN • MADRID
PRAGUE • WARSAW • BUDAPEST • AUCKLAND

ISBN 0-373-75053-6

ONE GOOD MAN

Copyright © 2005 by Charlotte Douglas.

www.eHarlequin.com

Printed in U.S.A.

ABOUT THE AUTHOR

The major passions of Charlotte Douglas's life are her husband—her high school sweetheart to whom she's been married for over three decades—and writing compelling stories. A national bestselling author, she enjoys filling her books with love of home and family, special places and happy endings. With their two cairn terriers, she and her husband live most of the year on Florida's central west coast, but spend the warmer months at their North Carolina mountaintop retreat.

No matter what time of year, readers can reach her at charlottedouglas1@juno.com. She's always delighted to hear from them.

Books by Charlotte Douglas

HARLEQUIN AMERICAN ROMANCE

HARLEQUIN INTRIGUE

*Identity Swap

Chapter One

Jeff Davidson eased deeper into the shadows of the gift shop. Thanks to his Special Operations experience, the former Marine shifted his six-foot-two, one-hundred-eighty pounds with undetectable stealth. But his military training offered no tactics to deal with the domestic firefight raging a few feet away.

With a stillness usually reserved for covert insertions into enemy territory, he peered through a narrow slit between the handmade quilts, rustic birdhouses and woven willow baskets that covered the shop's display shelves.

On the other side of the merchandise in the seating area of the café, a slender teenager with a cascade of straight, platinum hair yelled at her mother, her words exploding like a barrage from the muzzle of an M-16. "You are *so* not with it. Everyone I hang with has her navel pierced."

Jeff grimaced in silent disapproval. The kid should have her butt kicked, using that whiny, know-it-all tone toward her mom. Not that the girl's behavior was his business. He hadn't intended to eavesdrop. He'd come to Mountain Crafts and Café to talk business with Jodie Nathan, the owner, after her restaurant closed. Lingering until the staff left, he'd browsed the shelves of the gift section until she was alone.

But before he could make his presence known, fourteen-year-old Brittany had clattered down the stairs from their apartment over the store and confronted her mother.

"Your friends' navels are their mothers' concern, not mine." The struggle for calm was evident in Jodie's firm words, and the tired slump of her pretty shoulders suggested she'd waged this battle too many times. "You are my daughter, and as long as you live under my roof, you will follow my rules."

Was the kid blind? Jeff thought with disgust. Couldn't she see the tenderness and caring in her mother's remarkable hazel eyes? An ancient pain gnawed at his heart. He'd have given everything for such maternal love when he'd been a child, a teenager. Even now. Young Brittany Nathan had no idea how lucky she was.

"But, Mom—"

"You are *not* having your navel pierced, and that's final." This time Jodie failed to hide her exasperation.

"I hate you!" Brittany screamed.

The girl's lips, sporting almost-black lipstick, contorted in anger. Her green eyes, rimmed with heavy dark eyeliner, sparked fire, and her multiringed fingers clenched. Judging from her T-shirt, jeans and shoes, Jeff thought, black wasn't her favorite color. It was her only color.

She squared her thin shoulders for another assault. "Kimberly's mom lets her pierce whatever she wants."

"And if Kimberly wanted to jump off Devil's Mountain, I suppose her mother would let her." Weariness weighed Jodie's reply.

"I wish you weren't my mom!" Brittany aimed the words as if well aware of the wound they'd inflict. She pivoted on the heel of her clunky shoe, stomped out the front door and slammed it behind her.

Jeff started to leave his hiding spot but, at the stricken look on Jodie's face, decided to lay low and give her a minute to compose herself. The woman didn't deserve the grief her daughter had caused. Only thirty, Jodie had shocked the small town of Pleasant Valley, South Carolina, by becoming pregnant at fifteen. Instead of hiding the fact with an out-of-state abortion or giving up the child for adoption, she'd opted to raise her baby in Pleasant Valley, a gutsy move.

Jeff had been a senior in high school, an outcast in his own right, and he'd secretly identified with Jodie and the ostracism she'd suffered. The day after he graduated, he'd left town to join the Marines and hadn't laid eyes on Jodie since. He still hadn't gotten a really good look at her. Behind the lunch counter, she had folded her arms on its Formica surface and buried her head.

"Guess that disqualifies me as Mother of the Year," Jodie muttered loud enough for Jeff to hear, pain as prevalent as the irony in her voice.

Jeff couldn't detect sounds of crying. And remaining hidden would only add to his rudeness, so he stepped from behind the shelf and cleared his throat.

Jodie's head snapped up, and her enormous hazel eyes widened with alarm.

With his first face-to-face look, Jeff's breath caught in his chest. She wasn't the scrawny, freckle-faced kid he remembered. Jodie Nathan had grown into a knockout. Even with smudges of exhaustion beneath her eyes and her brown, sun-streaked hair tousled in disarray, her appearance was arresting: the delicate angles of her face reflected a maturity that added to her attractiveness; her feathery brows arched in obvious surprise; and her soft, sensuous mouth made a man think of long, deep kisses that led to more.

Her sage sweater showcased the proud set of her shoulders, braced as if for a blow, and her erect posture lifted small but exquisite breasts. The counter hid her from the waist down, but if the rest of her was as alluring, awkward little Jodie had blossomed into a woman who could turn men's heads, have a profound effect on lower parts of their anatomy. And break their hearts.

His own was hammering like a minigun, multibarrels firing. His penchant for coolness under fire shattered beneath her intense gaze.

"You heard?" she asked.

"Sorry." He finally found his voice. "I didn't mean to. I've been waiting to talk to you after the staff left."

Her eyes narrowed, and uneasiness flashed across her face. "Do I know you?"

"Jeff Davidson. It's been a while."

Jodie relaxed slightly at the familiar name, cocked her head and studied him. "You've changed."

"I'm older."

"It's more than age."

He grinned. "I've grown up, too. The Marines didn't tolerate blowhard delinquents."

"You wanted to talk to me?"

"A proposition."

Her expression hardened, and her enormous eyes glinted with anger. "Forget it. I wasn't that kind of girl when you left Pleasant Valley, and I'm not that kind of woman now."

"Whoa, back up." He held his hands palms outward as if warding off a blow. "I'm talking about a business deal."

The distrust in her eyes signaled her disbelief. "After observing my maternal ineptitude firsthand, you can't possibly think I can help with your home for troubled teens."

"Grant's told you about my project?"

She shook her head. "Merrilee Stratton keeps my darling brother too engrossed in wedding plans for long chats with his kid sister. But rumors about you and your project are flying all over town."

Jeff eyed her closely and detected no resentment when she spoke of her brother. Jodie was apparently happy about Grant's upcoming marriage. But her tone had changed when she'd mentioned rumors. If he read her correctly, hers wouldn't be the first negative attitude he'd encountered since returning home. Plenty of people would be glad to see Pleasant Valley's former bad boy fall on his face. And get out of town.

But Jodie's cooperation was crucial to his project. He couldn't let her refuse at the get-go. To ward off an initial turndown, he'd involve her gradually. Win her over slowly. And if he hit a snag maybe Grant could help grease the skids.

"If you have a few minutes," he said, "I'd like to fill you in on my plans."

With a frown that creased the perfect silken skin between her eyebrows, she hesitated. "If you're soliciting funds, you're wasting time. My own wayward teen has busted my budget."

Jeff shook his head. "It's a business deal, like I said. You'd be paid. If you're interested."

He'd kept his voice casual, as if her compliance didn't matter. He'd scare her off for sure if she knew how much he needed her help. Or how much more he wanted her involved, now that he'd had a good look at the grownup Jodie.

During his years as a Marine, Special Ops had been a man's job, and he'd encountered precious few women. The ones who had crossed his path had been either officers or foreign nationals, all off-limits. He'd lived like a monk, and he'd liked it that way. His work had required intense concentration. Sexual liaisons and emotional entanglements dulled a man's edge and might have gotten him or his team members killed.

But officers and foreigners belonged to his past. Jodie was his future and one hundred percent red-blooded American woman, the prettiest he'd ever seen. His long-suppressed interest soared.

"I can talk," she was saying, "but only a minute. Want some coffee? I have a fresh pot."

"Sounds good."

Jeff reined in his galloping imagination and focused on the job at hand. Since his return, he'd been met with mixed reactions in his hometown, everything from curiosity to encouragement to outright hostility. He wasn't certain exactly where Jodie's attitude fell on that continuum, but at least she hadn't cut him off without letting him speak, more than he could say for some folks.

As a teen growing up in this backwater town, his go-to-hell attitude had been a good cover against loneliness and his outcast status. As an adult, he struggled to overcome the residual effects of that rebellious past in order to succeed.

And he *wanted* success, not only for himself, but especially for the kids whose lives hung in the balance.

Jodie returned with two mugs of coffee and nodded toward a table at the front of the café. The closest to the door, he noted with wry amusement. In case she needed to bolt into the street.

"You afraid of me?" he asked.

"Should I be?" She settled into a seat across from him.

He swung his leg over a chair and sat. "Most people in town are."

She leaned her head to one side and studied him again, as if trying to make up her mind. Her incredible eyes, the irises a brilliant green rimmed with dark brown, didn't blink. "Some folks say the Marines turned you into a killing machine."

"And what do you say?"

"Did they?"

"Did I kill anyone?" He threw an internal wall around those grim memories, nightmares that sometimes haunted his sleep, and forced a grin. "That's classified, ma'am. If I told you—"

"You'd have to kill me?" She smiled at the tired old joke. "My brother says you're a good man. And Grant's usually right."

"Well, damn," Jeff said with an exaggerated

drawl, "and here I was, about to ask if you wanted anyone whacked. A decent reputation could ruin my future career as a hit man."

Her expression sobered for a second, as if she wondered if she'd misjudged him. Then, recognizing his teasing, she smiled, like the sun coming from behind a cloud. Only his deeply ingrained self-control kept him from laughing with delight at her beauty.

Her smile vanished as quickly at it had appeared and morphed into a no-nonsense look. "You mentioned a business proposition."

Detecting the skittishness beneath her poised facade, Jeff reminded himself to go slow, one phase at a time. "I need a caterer."

She shook her head. "I don't usually—"

"Grant told me." Jeff wouldn't give her time to refuse. "He also said your business has been slow and won't pick up till Memorial Day weekend."

"My brother talks too much."

"Cut him some slack," Jeff said. "He's a vet who works mainly with cows and horses. He needs interaction with people who can talk back."

"He has Merrilee."

"Lucky man," Jeff said with sincerity. "But before you turn me down, at least listen to what I have in mind. It's really simple."

"I'm listening." But she'd crossed her arms across those perfect breasts and leaned back in her chair, closing him out with her body language.

"We're having a dorm raising this weekend."

"We?"

"A group of my former Marine buddies. We're going to build a timber-frame dormitory for the camp. I need someone to provide food."

Jodie shook her head. "Maria Ortega's the only cook I have, and Saturday's a busy day at the café."

"I don't need a cook. Just someone to furnish sandwiches, drinks, and enough carbs to keep us going till the job's done."

"A few good men can't make their own sandwiches?" She raised one eyebrow.

"They could if I had time to plan and shop for groceries. But I'm up to my neck buying building supplies. I really need your help."

He could almost see the wheels turning behind those deep-enough-to-drown-in eyes. "Grant and Merrilee are coming to lend a hand," he added. "Maybe Merrilee could help you. I'll pay top dollar."

"How many to feed?"

"Eighteen, counting the framing crew, and they're all big eaters."

She rose and crossed the room, leaned over and removed something from beneath the counter. The movement pulled her green wool slacks taut across her slender hips and small bottom, a delectable sight. His mouth went dry.

She returned with a pad, pencil and calculator. "I'll figure on a variety of subs and potato salad. Chili, too, if the weather's cool. Several dozen cookies—chocolate chip, sugar, peanut butter—and some of Maria's famous cakes and pies. Iced tea and coffee.''

''Sounds great.''

''You haven't heard the price.'' She remained all business.

He clamped his teeth to keep from admitting that cost didn't matter. He could probably find someone else to provide food for his friends, but since seeing Jodie again, he wanted her more than ever as part of his special plans.

Man, that blow to the head in Afghanistan must have scrambled his senses. This was little Jodie Nathan, he reminded himself. Then why was he struggling to breathe, as if he'd just run a twenty-mile obstacle course with full gear?

''How much?'' he forced himself to ask.

She punched numbers into the calculator and named her price.

He tensed to keep his jaw from dropping. That much for subs and cookies? She'd obviously jacked up the cost in hopes he'd go elsewhere. But even if he didn't need her cooperation later, he would have agreed to the rip-off. He wanted Jodie there when his project started, because somehow she had suddenly become an integral part of his dream.

''It's a deal.'' He whipped out his checkbook, hastily wrote a check, and slid it across the table. He held out his hand to cinch the agreement.

Jodie blinked in surprise, but she took the check and grasped his hand with obvious reluctance. Hers felt small and delicate in his, but her grip was strong.

"Add doughnuts for a morning break," he said before releasing her. "And I'll need you on-site to serve and clean up."

Her eyes widened. "My being there wasn't part of the deal."

"At the price you quoted, you're well compensated for your time." He looked her squarely in the eyes. The younger Jodie he'd known had always been honest and trustworthy. A real Girl Scout. She knew she'd overcharged, and he guessed her conscience would force her to honor his conditions.

As if abruptly realizing he still held her hand, Jodie withdrew hers from his grasp.

Jeff shoved back from the table and stood. "I'll see you at eight o'clock Saturday morning at my place."

Jodie rose also. Her graceful movement called attention to her stunning figure, and he had to tear his gaze away. He strode to the door, opened it and turned to her.

"Pleasure doing business with you, ma'am." He didn't try to hide his smile. He'd won, and she knew it. He stepped outside and closed the door behind him.

JODIE SANK INTO HER CHAIR before her knees gave way. She rubbed damp palms on her slacks and drew a deep breath in a futile effort to calm her racing pulse. When Jeff had stepped from behind the display shelves, he'd looked like the epitome of every woman's dream. The perfect image for a Marine recruiting poster: tall, with broad shoulders, riveting gray eyes, neatly trimmed thick dark hair, a chiseled movie-star face marred only by a scar above his right cheekbone and a roguish smile with perfect teeth. And those muscles. Not a trace of flab. Just rock-hard strength. No wonder she hadn't recognized the lanky teenager from high school who'd always needed a haircut, a shave, clean clothes and a decent meal.

And that voice. Deep, commanding, mesmerizing. If he'd asked for anything more than catering, she didn't know if she could have resisted.

Her hands trembled and she clasped them together on the tabletop. What had he done to her? She hadn't felt this shaken since Randy Mercer had swaggered into her father's hardware store fifteen years ago. She groaned at the memory and laid her head on her hands. That time, two weeks later she was pregnant with Brittany.

God, she had to get a grip. She'd vowed never to let an attractive man overrule her good judgment again, and she'd managed just fine.

Until today.

Until Jeff Davidson had blasted in from the past, a gung-ho, kick-ass Marine who'd tossed her to the mat without so much as crooking a finger. She'd been certain that her exorbitant pricing would scare him off, but he hadn't even batted those incredibly long eyelashes at the outrageous figure she'd quoted. He'd merely smiled and caught her in her own trap. She should have just said no. Now she'd have to donate her excessive profit anonymously to his project to ease her guilty conscience.

She drew another deep breath. He'd taken her by surprise, that was all. Next time she'd be prepared to resist his good looks and charismatic charm. Such attributes could only lead to trouble. She wouldn't trade Brittany for anything, but Jodie had promised herself when her baby was born that she'd never, ever let her senses override her reason again.

Plenty of men had expressed an interest over the years. Jodie had briefly dated a few. But all had fallen short of the high standards she'd set after her first and only disastrous sexual experience. No one in Pleasant Valley had measured up to the qualities she admired in men, with the exception of her dad and her brother Grant, of course.

And none of the men she'd dated had exhibited the least interest in Brittany. Some had stated outright that the child was a deal-breaker in a relationship. So Jodie had remained single and happy. Men were definitely off her diet.

Her reaction to Jeff had been a fluke. It wouldn't happen again.

She pushed to her feet, dismayed to find her legs still shaky, grabbed the coffee mugs from the tabletop and headed for the counter. While tucking his check into the cash register, she glimpsed Jeff out front astride his vintage Harley and talking to a police-woman. A satisfied smile tugged at the corners of her mouth. She hoped Officer Brynn Sawyer was giving him a ticket. Serve the handsome devil right.

She had stowed the mugs in the dishwasher when the bell over the door tinkled. Afraid Jeff had come back, she felt her pulse rev and her face flush. When she turned, however, it was only Brynn.

"You're still in uniform." Jodie hoped Brynn wouldn't notice her reddened face, although the officer, trained to observe, never missed much. "Didn't your shift end hours ago?"

Brynn perched on a stool at the counter. "I've been catching up on paperwork."

"Want coffee?"

Brynn nodded. Even in her severely cut blue uniform, the tall, shapely woman with dark auburn hair was a knockout. Men had been known to exceed speed limits merely for the pleasure of being pulled over by Pleasant Valley's gorgeous cop. Brynn, how-ever, remained unaware of her beauty. She was too married to her job to pay attention to much else, especially the gaggle of admiring guys who often hovered around her. Totally focused, she performed her duties with above-and-beyond devotion. Everyone in town felt safer with Brynn on patrol.

"I've got some new material," Brynn said, a twinkle lighting her midnight-blue eyes.

"Not more lawyer jokes, please," Jodie said with a fake groan and filled her coffee mug.

Brynn had a thing about lawyers. And Yankees. Otherwise generous and open-minded to a fault, Jodie's friend couldn't tolerate either as a group. But if an individual attorney or Northerner needed help, Brynn was there in a New York minute.

"How many of those lawyer jokes do you know?" Jodie said.

"Only three." Brynn's grin was wicked. "The rest are true stories."

Jodie couldn't help laughing. Brynn always cheered her up, even after her worst rows with Brittany.

Brynn dumped artificial sweetener and cream in her coffee and stirred. "How does a pregnant woman know she's carrying a future lawyer?"

"There's no stopping you, is there?"

Her friend's grin widened. "She has an uncontrollable craving for baloney. What does a lawyer use for birth control?"

"I give up."

"His personality." She barely paused for breath. "What happens when you cross a pig with a lawyer?"

Jodie laughed. "I'm afraid to ask."

"Nothing. There're some things even a pig won't do. What do you call—"

"Stop, please." Jodie struggled to speak through her laughter. "Is this how you interrogate suspects? Lawyer-joke them until they crack?"

"Now there's a thought." Brynn cut her a probing glance. "Guess you saw Jeff Davidson."

"He has a catering job for me." Jodie worked to keep her tone casual.

"You don't do catering."

Jodie shrugged. "I do now."

"For the dorm raising?"

"How'd you know?"

"I'm invited."

"You? You're more tool challenged than I am. Unless we're talking guns, of course." Brynn was a crack shot who'd won several competitions. But, as far as Jodie knew, the officer had never fired her weapon on the job.

"I don't have to work Saturday," Brynn said. "And Jeff thinks my presence will lend respectability to his project. If I witness what's happening, I can combat rumors."

"So he worked his devilish charm on you, too?"

"Devilish charm?" Brynn gave her a blank look.

Being a cop must have inoculated her friend against male charisma, especially since so many men Brynn encountered were felons. Jeff had come close to that category in high school, Jodie remembered.

Brynn's face lit with sudden comprehension. "Charm? Sister Jodie, our resident nun, found Jeff *charming?*"

"Of course not, but he tried to use his wiles with me."

"If you didn't find him charming, why are you catering for him?" Brynn, an expert at gauging reactions, was watching her every move.

Jodie was determined to appear unaffected by the Marine's appeal. "Because he agreed to pay the outrageous price I quoted."

Brynn wrinkled her nose. "Why do you suppose he did that?"

"Because he's desperate?"

"He could feed his crew of Marines beef jerky and water and they wouldn't complain. Maybe he fell for *your* charms."

"Don't be silly." Jodie picked up a cloth, scrubbed a non-existent stain on the spotless counter and changed the subject. "I had another row with Brittany."

Brynn sighed. "What's she done now?"

"Wants her navel pierced."

"Best place. Least defacing. Least visible."

Jodie snorted. "Not the way she dresses. Besides, it's a precedent. First the navel, then an eyebrow, then…" She stopped and shuddered. "I don't know what to do, Brynn. She's slipping away from me, becoming more rebellious and angry each day. And with her wild, out-of-control friends, she's headed for more trouble.''

''I checked out the names you gave me. None of these kids have been arrested. Not like the last group.''

Jodie shook her head. ''Maybe they just haven't been caught.''

''Maybe you should get married.''

Jodie had taken a sip of coffee and almost spewed it. ''What?''

''Brittany needs a father figure.'' Brynn said matter-of-factly. ''And you could use a husband.''

''She has father figures. Her grandpa Nathan and her uncle Grant.''

''And you have?''

The perfect comeback. ''I have my job. Just like you.''

''Touché.'' Brynn chugged her coffee. ''I'll give you a hand Saturday, since I'll be at the dorm raising anyway.''

''Want to ride with Brittany and me?''

''You're taking Brit?''

''She's been working Saturdays with Grant at the clinic. But he's going to the dorm raising, too.'' Jodie sighed. ''I don't dare leave her unsupervised for a full day. Who knows the trouble she'd get into.''

''I'd better take my own vehicle. And my radio. In case I get a call.''

''All work and no play—''

"Isn't that the second verse of the song I just sang for you?"

Before Jodie could reply, Brynn downed the rest of her coffee.

"Gotta go," she said. "See you around."

Jodie followed and locked the door behind her. Her visit with Brynn had grounded her and brought her raging hormones under control. Her reaction to Jeff Davidson had been a fluke. Come Saturday, feeding a horde of hungry men and keeping an eye on Brittany, Jodie could play her ice maiden role again with no problem.

Piece of cake.

She climbed the stairs and ignored the niggling reminder that a piece of cake was the first step in falling off a years-long diet.

Chapter Two

On Saturday, Jodie crawled reluctantly out of her warm bed before dawn. She'd worked past midnight preparing subs, making potato salad, baking cookies and gathering paper goods. With Saturday's forecast high in the upper fifties, she'd also started two Crock-Pots of chili. Groggy from too little sleep, she stowed the food and supplies in her minivan and awakened her daughter.

Brittany dressed, muttered complaints all the way to the car and instantly fell asleep in the front seat.

Jodie considered her dozing daughter with a tenderness that brought moisture to her eyes. It seemed only yesterday that Brittany, a tiny precious bundle with blond ringlets and a delightful baby gurgle, had required the child carrier in the back seat. Only weeks instead of years since Jodie had piled Brittany and her nine-year-old teammates into the van for soccer practices. What had turned her once loving and adorable daughter so rebellious, so bitter? Did adolescence with its hormonal fluctuations and resulting emotional roller coaster make all teens this difficult?

Or had Jodie, as Brittany so often implied, failed as a parent?

Failed? How could she not? She'd been a kid herself when Brittany was born.

Shoving that thought away before it ruined her whole day, she debated waking Brittany to share the breathtaking sunrise over the beautiful farming valley from which the town took its name.

Jodie drove the familiar route at a comfortable speed, and the van hugged the narrow highway that meandered alongside the Piedmont River, broad and tranquil in some spots, in others a torrent of white water over a boulder-strewn bed. Slanting, dawn sunlight glinted off the spring green of willows, oaks and maples, struggling toward full leaf in mid-May. On either side of the river, rolling pastures lush with high grass and freshly plowed acreage stretched toward the haze-draped mountains that surrounded the valley like the sides of a bowl.

Jodie rounded a curve and passed the veterinary clinic where Grant and his future father-in-law, Jim Stratton, worked as partners. Their trucks already stood in the parking lot, because the vets' day began with the farmers', long before dawn.

Brittany awakened, crossed her arms, and set her face in its customary scowl. "Why do I have to come? I had plans with my friends."

Exactly why you're with me, cupcake. Brittany's current pals gave Jodie nightmares. "I need your help."

"Who is this Jeff Davidson?"

"A friend of your uncle Grant."

"Huh," Brittany said with a snort of disdain. "I didn't know Uncle Grant hung with lowlifes."

Jodie cast her a sharp glance. "Who said Jeff's a lowlife?"

"The whole town knows he was no good."

"Jeff had a tough time growing up."

"Yeah, tell me about it."

Jodie silently counted to ten. Her daughter had become a travel agent for first-class guilt trips. "Jeff's father, Hiram, was a lowlife, no doubt about it. Never held a job and stayed stinking drunk his entire adult life. He was locked up so often Chief Sawyer named a cell after him."

Brittany studied her black-painted fingernails without comment.

Jodie couldn't tell if the girl's boredom was real or feigned. "Jeff's mother died when he was a baby."

"Who took care of him?"

Ah, a note of interest from the blasé Miss Brittany? Would wonders never cease?

"His drunken father," Jodie said. "It's a miracle Jeff survived. When he was old enough, his father forced him to make moonshine deliveries."

"Moonshine? Yuck." Brittany made a face.

Jodie hoped her daughter's response wasn't based on personal experience. "Hiram ran a still somewhere on the mountain behind their house."

Like a camera flash, a memory flared of Jeff, long dark hair blowing in the wind, black leather jacket zipped to his chin, roaring through town on his Harley, its saddlebags filled with Mason jars of white lightning cushioned with moss. The boy had been arrogant. Solitary. Lonely. With a don't-come-close-or-I'll-break-you-in-two expression.

Brittany squirmed in her seat. "Will his father be at the farm today?"

"Hiram died a year ago."

Brittany was silent for a moment. "Anybody my age coming?"

"Not today."

Lordy, Jodie hoped not. She had enough trouble with Brittany's current friends. She definitely didn't want her daughter fraternizing with Jeff's clients, kids within a hair's breadth of going to jail for a long, long time.

Reality check.

When Grant had first told her of Jeff's project, a camp to rehabilitate potentially prison-bound teens, she'd been caught up in her brother's enthusiasm.

"If Jeff hadn't joined the Marines right out of high school," Grant had explained, "he might have ended up in jail himself. So he understands where these kids are coming from. And where they might be headed."

Good for Jeff Davidson, Jodie had thought. But now, considering her impressionable teenage daughter, the last thing Jodie wanted for her was more bad influences. And Jeff's rehabilitation project would bring trouble to Pleasant Valley literally by the busload.

Jodie gripped the wheel to keep from smacking herself upside the head. Here she was, aiding and abetting, providing food and comfort to the enemy. What the heck had she been thinking?

Damn Jeff Davidson and his Marine-recruiting-poster charm. Thanks to her scrambled senses when he'd caught her by surprise, she hadn't been thinking at all.

But Jeff wouldn't have clients yet, she assured herself. The dorm wasn't built, so the teens didn't have a place to stay. And, thank God, the Davidson place was at the opposite end of the valley from town. When Jeff's delinquents did arrive, they'd be too far away to interact with Brittany.

Jodie forced herself to relax. She and Brittany would feed Jeff's building crew and take off. Her daughter would have no further contact with Jeff or his camp. For Brittany's sake, Jodie didn't want the rehabilitation facility in Pleasant Valley, but she remained open-minded enough to avoid the not-in-my-backyard syndrome. Jeff's teens needed help. A nasty job, but somebody had to do it.

So long as the program didn't affect her already problematic daughter, Jodie would file no objections.

She reached the end of the valley and headed the van up the winding road, a series of switchbacks that worked their way up the steep mountainside. Halfway up, she turned onto a gravel road, almost hidden by arching branches of rhododendron ready to burst into bloom. Heavy dew clung to white clusters of mountain laurel and bowed the heavily leafed branches of the hardwood forest. Jodie observed the unfamiliar route with interest. She'd never visited the Davidson farm and knew the way only from Grant's directions.

Brittany peered through the shadows cast by the trees. "Are you sure this is the right road? We're in the middle of nowhere."

Jodie was also wondering if she was lost when a clearing opened ahead. She stopped the van at its edge and surveyed the Davidson property. Unlike the fertile farmland of the valley, this terrain was rugged and rocky. The only structures were a run-down farmhouse, a ramshackle barn, its unpainted boards weathered gray, and a few outbuildings. To one side of the barn, a terrace had been carved out of the hillside long ago, a space barely big enough for a vegetable garden, a pond and a tiny pasture.

On the opposite side of the farmhouse, a larger terrace had been graded recently, judging by the bare red clay. Stacks of lumber lay beside a huge concrete-block foundation, and beyond, a driver on a track-hoe worked the land, enlarging the level surface one buck-etful of hard clay and rocks at a time.

Brittany sat up straighter and peered out the wind-shield with interest. "Where's the still?"

Jodie eased the van beside Brynn's car in front of the farmhouse and shut off the engine. "Destroyed. After his father died, Jeff told the authorities where to find it."

"Where does Jeff—"

"Mr. Davidson, to you, kiddo."

Brittany heaved a sigh. "Where does he get the money for all this?"

Out of the mouths of babes, Jodie thought. Hiram Davidson never had two nickels to rub together, and Marine pay hadn't made Jeff rich. How *was* Jeff pay-ing for his project?

She started to comment, but Jeff bounded out the door of the farmhouse and sprinted down the steps toward them. Every bit of breath left her body in a whoosh.

With his killer smile flashing, he was dressed in khaki cargo shorts that revealed muscular, tanned legs, lace-up workboots with wool socks, a cable-knit sweater in olive drab and a soft cap with USMC em-blazoned across the front in proud gold letters. At ease, but with an underlying alertness that could snap to attention in a millisecond, he looked handsome enough for a starring role on one of Jodie's favorite television programs.

Move over, JAG Commander Harmon Rabb, and be still my heart.

Jodie took a deep breath to clear her head. She was thirty years old, a mother and a businesswoman. She had to stop reacting to the man as if she were some teenage Marine Corps groupie.

Four similarly attired men came out of the house behind Jeff and waited on the porch.

"Holy beefcake," Brittany murmured.

"And all old enough to be your father," Jodie said sharply. Instantly she wanted to snatch the words back. Of all the sore spots between them, the subject of Brittany's father was the touchiest.

Jodie unfastened her seat belt and climbed out of the car. She had to have air. An unaccustomed heat flooded her. Hormones. Had to be. Did having a baby at fifteen precipitate early menopause? What else would throw her body into hot flashes?

Brittany left the car and joined her as Jeff reached them.

"You're right on time." His gaze, deep-gray eyes that seemed almost black, locked with hers.

For an instant time stood still and she forgot to breathe.

He turned to her daughter and broke the spell. "You must be Brittany. I'm Jeff."

"Mr. Davidson, Brittany." Jodie reminded her daughter. She'd raised her to treat grown-ups with respect. She wouldn't let anyone undermine her efforts. Not even the world's most attractive former Marine.

"Hi…sir." Brittany looked ready to dig a hole and climb in.

Jodie groaned inwardly. Everything she did further alienated the girl.

"Your mom would make a good Marine." Jeff turned his charm on Brittany, and she actually smiled.

"Only if she's an officer," Brittany said with the air of a conspirator. "She's good at giving orders."

"That means she loves you," Jeff said. "Take it from someone who knows. My old man never gave a…hoot what I did."

Jodie blinked in surprise. Jeff had taken her side, and not only hadn't Brittany bristled, she was still smiling.

Jeff's friends joined them, and he offered introductions. "Jodie and Brittany Nathan, meet my team."

A tall and solidly built man with pale-blue eyes, ruddy cheeks and hair like corn silk offered Jodie his hand. "I'm Gofer, ma'am."

After squeezing Jodie's fingers in a crushing grip, he took Brittany's hand.

"Hi, Mr. Gofer," Brittany said. Jodie's lesson on manners had apparently taken hold.

Gofer laughed. "My real name's Jack Hager. My team calls me Gofer."

Brittany cast Jodie a what-do-I-do-now look.

Before Jodie could respond, Jeff said, "We call

him Gofer because 'go-fer-broke' is his favorite expression.''

A rugged man with deep black skin, broad shoulders, and a close-shaved head shook Jodie's hand next. ''Kermit. Pleased to meet you, ma'am.''

''That's your real name?'' Jodie asked.

Kermit laughed with a rumbling sound deep in his broad chest and showed fine white teeth. ''No, ma'am. It's a nickname, too.''

Brittany, who'd been a huge Sesame Street fan as a toddler, asked, ''Like Kermit the Frog?''

Kermit's smile widened. ''That's the one.''

''Every time we pulled on our BDUs—'' Gofer began.

''Battle dress uniforms,'' Jeff explained.

''And smeared on camou-paint,'' Gofer continued, ''he sang, 'It Isn't Easy Being Green.' So we call him Kermit.''

''And this is Ricochet.'' Jeff pointed to a lanky fellow with soft brown eyes and curly brown hair who was nearly as tall as Jeff himself.

''Ma'am,'' he responded with a respectful nod. ''Brittany.''

''We call him Ricochet,'' Gofer, apparently the most talkative of the group, explained, ''because he can't keep still.''

Had Ricochet actually blushed, Jodie wondered, or was his color a trick of the rising sun?

"Unless we're on a mission," Jeff added. "Then he's as focused as a hound on a ham bone."

"And I'm Trace, Ms. Nathan." The fourth member of the team was tall and muscular with long, slender hands and the face of a poet. "Short for Tracey, my last name."

"What do they call you, Mr. Davidson?" Brittany asked.

As one body, the four men snapped to attention and shouted in one voice, "Lieutenant Davidson, sir!"

"At ease," Jeff ordered with a laugh. "And help these ladies unload their car."

Jodie swallowed her astonishment. Outcast Jeff Davidson, whom everyone had believed would join Hell's Angels and die in a bar fight, was an officer and a gentleman? Who would have thought?

Jeff motioned toward the building site. "We set up tables under a canopy and ran a power source. Having the food nearby will speed up our work."

Jodie opened the van's hatch. Kermit and Gofer each grabbed a Crock-Pot, Trace manhandled the massive coffeemaker she'd borrowed from the church, and Ricochet tucked a huge cooler under each arm and headed for the tables. Jeff began stacking boxes of baked goods.

"Where's Brynn?" Jodie asked. "I see her car."

"Inside." Jeff used his chin to steady the pile of boxes in his arms. "With Daniel."

"Another member of your team?"

"Nope," Jeff called over his shoulder as he followed the other men. "My first client. He's living with me until the dorm's finished."

"Cool," Brittany said. "Can I meet him?"

"Not now. I need your help." Jodie winced at the edge to her voice.

She definitely had her work cut out for her. Between feeding ravenous Marines and keeping her daughter away from Jeff's first resident delinquent, it was going to be a long day.

FIVE HOURS LATER Jeff sat beneath a sugar maple and devoured a bowl of chili and an Italian sub. The morning had gone well. The timber framing crew from Asheville had arrived immediately after Jodie. Grant and Merrilee had made a brief appearance but had to leave when the vet received an emergency call.

With Jeff and his buddies, assisted by Brynn and Daniel providing additional grunt work, the massive dormitory with kitchen/dining/living room was taking shape. By dark, the framing would be complete, and Jeff and his Marines could add the roof, walls and finishing work over the next few weeks.

An unaccustomed lump blocked his throat. He'd never had friends while growing up in Pleasant Valley, mostly due to his father's infamous reputation. Jeff hadn't been like the other kids with their extended families, tidy homes with white picket fences and fathers who didn't stay raging drunk and beat the crap out of them. And no one had understood better than Jeff that he didn't belong. He'd built a wall around himself merely to survive.

But the corps had been different. Backgrounds and social status were irrelevant. All that mattered was that a man carried his load, became part of the team and watched his buddies' backs. Determined to make the grade, Jeff had thrown himself first into training and later into missions with every fiber of his being. As gung-ho, kick-ass, hang-tough as the best of them, he'd not only developed self-esteem, he'd won the unqualified respect and undying loyalty of his men. And he loved them more than he'd loved his own blood kin.

"Dessert?" A soft, musical voice interrupted his thoughts.

Jeff glanced up at Jodie, standing in front of him with a plate of chocolate cake in each hand. He set aside his empty chili bowl and wiped his mouth with a paper napkin. "If you'll join me."

Her creamy complexion blushed like a Georgia peach. "I have to—"

"You've served everyone else. They're fine."

Jodie glanced across the clearing as if hoping to prove him wrong, but the framing crew, gathered at the back of their pickups, held full plates. Brynn, flanked by Brittany and Daniel, sat under the canopy at a makeshift table of planks and sawhorses. Gofer and Kermit had set up a chessboard on a nearby stump and were engrossed in a game. Picking up trash and stray tools and, as usual, unable to stay in one place, Ricochet wandered the work site. Trace reclined on the porch steps with his nose in a novel, *Cold Mountain,* whose namesake stood just over the North Carolina line near the Blue Ridge Parkway, fifty miles north.

Jeff patted the ground beside him. "Sit with me."

With the tension of a wild animal trapped with no place to run, Jodie handed him a plate and sank beside him.

"I won't bite," he said.

"Hmmmph." She avoided his eyes. "Thought you Marines ate civilians for lunch."

He lifted the plate with its thick wedge of cake. "Only when there aren't such delicious alternatives."

Not that Jodie wasn't delicious in her own way. The delicate fragrance of her magnolia-scented shampoo teased his nostrils and fanned a hunger unrelated to food. He stowed his desire and put a lock on it. He had promises to keep, and no woman, not even one as pretty as Jodie, could distract him.

"You have a name for this place?" she asked.

Jeff shrugged. "I've always called it home, such as it is."

"I mean your project, your camp. It has to have a name."

He'd named it, all right. Maybe if Jodie knew the

story behind that name, she'd be more amenable to helping later. "I'm calling it Archer Farm."

"Archer? As in bows and arrows?" She seemed confused.

"Archer, as in Captain Colin Archer," Jeff said quietly, steeled against the pain the name evoked.

"One of your team?" She indicated the Marines scattered across the building site.

"The best of our team, but he's not here today. Except in spirit."

Jodie took a bite of chocolate cake and waited for him to continue.

"Arch saved my life in Afghanistan."

Remembering, Jeff could almost feel the biting cold of that winter night, see the star-strewn heavens above the dark mountain peaks, taste the grit of the desert and hear the keening wind.

"We were on a re-con mission to identify the exact location of a terrorist group hiding in a complex of connected caves. Our job was to secure coordinates, convey them to headquarters and get out. Smart bombs would do the rest.

"Harris and I took point, and, in spite of all precautions, Harris somehow tripped a land mine."

Jodie set her cake aside, as if her appetite had fled.

"Harris died instantly," Jeff said, "and I was injured. Couldn't move. Men with guns poured out of those caves like a scene from a Schwarzenegger movie. Only all too real."

Jodie shuddered, drew her knees to her chest and hugged them.

"The team tossed smoke grenades and laid down covering fire. Arch fought his way through and carried me out."

"Must have been scary," Jodie said.

"Scary is too mild a term. I was terrified out of my mind."

"Captain Archer must have been, too."

Jeff nodded. "People have the wrong idea about courage. Bravery doesn't mean you're not afraid. It means doing what you have to, in spite of your fears."

"So you're naming your project after the man who saved your life?"

"He did more than that. Arch went back after Harris."

"But Harris was dead."

"Marines don't leave their men behind. Ever."

"So Archer was a hero twice over that night."

"He was more than a hero. He was my best friend, the closest thing to a brother I ever had." Jeff took a bite of cake and forced himself to swallow past the tightness in his throat. The creamy chocolate tasted like dust and ashes.

"Was?"

"He was killed a year later by a suicide bomber in Baghdad. I'd have been with him if I hadn't been in sick bay with food poisoning."

"I'm sorry about your friend."

Bitterness consumed him. "Hell of a way for Arch to die. The bravest man I know killed by a fanatical coward." Jeff shook his head in disgust, using anger to hold back tears. "He should be here today. This project was our dream."

"You've been planning this a long time?"

"Ever since Arch and I met in boot camp. He came from a tough Chicago neighborhood, an orphan raised by his elderly grandmother. The Marine Corps was his ticket out, same as mine."

"But you came back here."

Jeff nodded. "Arch and I agreed that once we left the service, we'd build this place together. We wanted to help other troubled kids before they were swallowed up by the legal system and sent to prison."

"Kids like Daniel?" Jodie's voice sounded strange, as if under tight control.

Jeff nodded. "I took Daniel, even though the dorm's not ready. He'll live with me until it is."

"Why the hurry?"

Jeff wished he could read her better. Her expression gave nothing away, and he couldn't tell if she was sympathetic or merely polite.

"Because Daniel was only days from being sentenced to an adult correctional facility. One he'd never survive."

"What did he do?" Jodie's question held an agitated note.

"He's a smart kid who made stupid mistakes."

"They don't lock you up for being stupid," she said with a tinge of sarcasm. "What was he charged with?"

Jeff sighed. From the harshness in her voice, he'd apparently lost the battle for Jodie's support, but a Marine didn't quit. He wouldn't concede the war. Not yet.

"Shoplifting," he admitted with reluctance. "Grand theft auto, resisting arrest and assault on a police officer."

Jodie gasped. "Does Brynn know?"

Jeff looked across the yard where Brynn laughed with Brittany and Daniel over their desserts. "She's Archer Farm's law enforcement liaison. She'll have files on all our clients."

Jodie stood abruptly. "Excuse me. I have to speak with my daughter."

Disappointed, Jeff watched her hurry away. Jodie Nathan with her Mountain Crafts and Café had exactly the resources Archer Farm needed to succeed. He could probably locate other help, but he doubted he'd find anyone he wanted to work with as much as Jodie.

Chapter Three

Jodie forced herself not to run. More than anything, she wanted to snatch Brittany from Daniel's presence, shove her in the car and take off, as fast and far from Archer Farm as Jodie could drive.

But she knew better. She was no expert in teen psychology, but she'd learned enough. If Brittany even suspected her mother didn't want her at Archer Farm, Jeff's project would become her daughter's most desirable destination.

Jodie wanted to stop, scream and shake her fists at the heavens. Why, every time her sex drive kicked in, did her brain check out? What kind of spell had Jeff Davidson cast that she'd allowed herself to become involved with his plans? Between Brittany and the business, Jodie already had her hands full. She didn't need more temptations dangled in front of her very impressionable child, and she particularly didn't need the distraction of a man as good-looking and compassionate as Jeff.

Anger and frustration threatened to strangle her. Being a single mom was hard enough. Why did Jeff have to add to her problems by bringing his jail-bound teens to Pleasant Valley? Why not Chicago where his pal Archer had come from?

Hard to farm in Chicago, logic reminded her.

Jodie wasn't operating on logic, however, but pure, unadulterated maternal instinct. Jeff's clients posed a potential threat to her child, and Jodie pledged every effort to keep Brittany away.

But Jeff also threatened Jodie's well-ordered single life in a way no other man had. She liked him, he was interesting, he made her pulse race and she wanted to spend more time with him. Which was exactly why she vowed to keep herself away from Jeff and Archer Farm, as well.

Slowing her steps to a casual saunter, she approached the table where Brynn sat with Brittany and Jeff's first client.

"How many lawyers," Brynn was saying, "does it take to change a lightbulb?"

"How many?" Brittany said.

"Three. One to climb the ladder, one to shake the ladder, and one to sue the ladder company."

Brittany and Daniel laughed, until they took a look at Jodie's face. Brittany's laughter died in her throat, and Daniel shoved to his feet.

Well, well. A felon with manners.

Even as she thought it, Jodie recognized she wasn't

being fair. Daniel didn't look like a hardened criminal. Thin and tall, with his freckles, wide blue eyes, shaggy hair that needed cutting, and deer-in-the-headlights expression, he reminded her of a scared little kid who wanted his mother. And he couldn't be many days over sixteen.

Dear God, why was life so complicated? Why couldn't the bad guys look like bad guys?

Jodie inhaled deeply, forced herself to relax and smile. "I see you haven't exhausted your repertoire," she said to Brynn.

Her friend, looking especially ravishing out of uniform in snug-fitting jeans, leather boots and a sweatshirt that brought out the dark blue in her eyes, grinned. "I haven't even started on my Yankee jokes."

Jodie groaned, rolled her eyes and sat. She'd wait until the crews started back to work after lunch, ask Brittany to help load the car and leave. Their departure would seem natural then, instead of the panicked flight she wanted this very moment.

"Tell us, Aunt Brynn." Brittany adored her mother's friend, who, unlike Jodie, could do no wrong in her daughter's eyes.

Brynn didn't need encouragement. "A young man from the Smoky Mountains studied very hard all his life and won a full scholarship to a prestigious Ivy League college in New England. He'd never left home before, and he soon lost his way on the large campus.

"So he stopped an older student and asked in his slow mountain drawl, 'Could you please tell me where the library's at?'"

Daniel and Brittany exchanged amused glances at Brynn's exaggerated twang.

"The older student looked down his nose with a sneer at the newcomer and replied in clipped Yankee tones, 'If you spoke proper English, you would know *never* to end a sentence with a preposition.'

"The mountaineer grinned. 'Of course. Thank you kindly for the grammar lesson. Now, will you please tell me where the library's at, jack—'"

"Brynn!" Jodie interrupted sharply, but Brittany and Daniel caught the officer's drift and howled with laughter.

"Sorry," Brynn said. "I hang around cops too much." She turned to Brittany. "That language is not appropriate for a young lady. And you, Daniel, must be especially cautious of how you speak. You need to make the best impression possible, understand?"

"Yes, ma'am," the boy agreed with a respectful nod.

The sound of an engine straining on an uphill grade broke the silence, and a delivery truck from the local builders' supply rumbled into the clearing.

Across the yard, Jeff jumped to his feet. "Let's help unload."

"Ooo-rah!" his team answered in unison and double-timed it to the truck. Daniel and Brittany got up and joined them.

"Get the feeling those guys would follow Jeff to hell and back?" Brynn asked.

"From what he's told me, they already have," Jodie said quietly and watched the men heft heavy timbers onto their shoulders as if they weighed no more than matchsticks.

"Is that why you looked so spooked a minute ago? Too many war stories?"

Jodie shook her head. "I'm worried about Brit, and I'm taking her home as soon as I can. Daniel has a rap sheet as long as my arm. She shouldn't be around him."

"He needs a friend, Jodie."

"Someone else's daughter can be his friend."

"Aren't you being harsh?"

"The boy's jail-bound. I don't want him steering Jodie in the same direction."

Brynn shook her head. "I've seen his rap sheet. And I've read between the lines. He's a good boy who fell in with the wrong crowd. Did the wrong things for the right reasons. Otherwise the judge would have made Daniel reservations at the Gray Bar Inn, not here."

"The Gray Bar Inn?" Jodie couldn't help smiling. "Are you never serious?"

"I am now." Brynn's expression backed up her

words. "Give him a chance, Jodie. If people turn their backs on Daniel, he'll believe he's no good, and then he's truly lost."

"What about Brittany?"

"Cut her some slack. You've instilled good values in her. She knows what to do."

Jodie wished she had Brynn's certainty, but said no more, because Jeff had apparently assured the teens they weren't needed, and Brittany and Daniel were returning to the table.

"Mom, Daniel says there's a creek up the mountain that's full of tadpoles. Can we check it out?"

Jodie bit back the *no* that sprang instantly to her lips and met Brynn's pleading gaze. "Okay, but stay within shouting distance. We'll be leaving soon."

With whoops of delight, the teens turned and raced like children toward the worn footpath that led into the forest behind the farmhouse.

Jodie sank onto a bench. "I hope I'm not making a mistake."

"I'll wander up and check on them in a few minutes," Brynn promised.

Jodie stowed the empty Crock-Pots in the van, but left the remaining food in coolers. As hard as the men were working, they'd be hungry again soon. True to her word, Brynn followed the teens up the mountain. Ricochet's cleanup left Jodie nothing to do, so she returned to the bench beneath the canopy and watched the massive dorm take shape.

The framers and Marines were manhandling the roof trusses, when one of the heavy beams slipped and landed a glancing blow on Gofer's foot. A blue streak, a virtuoso performance of profanity, colored the air, and, in addition to her concern for the man's injury, Jodie was glad Brittany was out of earshot.

"Got a first-aid kit?" she called.

"On the porch," Jeff directed.

With his arms around Jeff and Kermit's shoulders, Gofer hobbled toward the canopy.

Jodie ran across the yard and up the porch steps, grabbed the kit and returned to the canopy. Jeff and Kermit had eased Gofer to a bench, and Jeff was removing his buddy's boot.

"Guess I owe the pot a fortune," Gofer said between gritted teeth.

Jeff nodded but didn't take his eyes from the injured foot. "At a dollar a word, to use your favorite expression, I'd say you went for broke."

Gofer drew in a breath that hissed between his teeth and looked up at Jodie. "The team's trying to clean up its vocabulary, to set an example for our teens."

Kermit hovered, looking over Jeff's shoulder to assess the damage to Gofer's foot. "We made a pact," he explained to Jodie, "a dollar a word for any curses. Gofer, old bud, you just filled the jar. That fu...dging foot must be hurting like...heck."

"I'm okay," Gofer grumbled. "I don't want to

slow you guys down. The framers quit at four whether the damn, uh darn thing's done or not.''

Jeff stood. ''The building can wait until I'm sure you're okay.''

''I'll take care of him,'' Jodie offered.

''Yeah,'' Gofer said, ''she makes a much prettier nurse than you, Lieutenant.''

Jeff paused and studied Gofer as if to assure himself the man would be all right.

''Thanks, Jodie.'' Jeff threw her a look that melted her insides, and, with Kermit, hurried back to the site to help retrieve the fallen truss.

Jodie knelt in front of Gofer and gingerly finished removing his bloody sock. ''No wonder you swore. The beam split your big toe. You ought to have stitches.''

''Just a scratch, ma'am,'' the Marine said without wincing, although his face had the pinched look of a person in agony. ''I've had worse.''

Jodie cleaned the wound with peroxide, slathered it with an antibiotic cream that also killed pain and bandaged the toe. ''You should stay off it.''

She expected protests, but Gofer merely nodded in agreement, and leaned back, elbows on the table, breathing hard. ''You an old friend of the lieutenant's?''

Jodie recognized that he was trying to focus on something besides his throbbing foot.

''Jeff's several years older than me.'' She couldn't

admit that the man whose team worshiped him like a hero hadn't had any friends. "He graduated high school with my brother."

"The vet I met this morning?"

Jodie nodded. "Archer Farm's going to keep Grant busy. Jeff has quite a menagerie."

"Horses, goats, cows, chickens, ducks and pigs. For the teens to take care of. Teaches 'em responsibility. Might even teach some of them how to love."

"You a psychiatrist?" Jodie asked with a smile.

"Psychologist," Gofer answered.

"Really? They taught you that in the Marines?"

He shook his head. "I'd almost finished graduate school when I decided to fight terrorism. I immediately joined the Marines. After leaving the service last year, I completed my Ph.D. And signed on with Jeff as Archer Farm's resident counselor."

While talking with Gofer, Jodie had observed Jeff leaving the work site and disappearing into the woods behind the house. He returned with Brynn in tow and approached Gofer.

"Officer Sawyer's going to drive you into town, Gofer," Jeff said. "You could have broken bones. I want that foot X-rayed."

"No need, sir. I'm fine."

Brynn placed her fists on her hips. "You resisting an officer, soldier?"

Gofer looked from Brynn's determined expression

to the set of Jeff's firm jaw and grinned. "You're an officer who's hard to resist, ma'am."

"Please, call me Brynn. Or Officer Sawyer. Anything but ma'am. It makes me feel old."

Gofer's grin split his face. "You don't have to worry about age, ma'am."

"Want a couple of guys to carry you to the car?" Jeff asked.

"If Brynn will give me a hand," Gofer said, "I can manage."

He pushed gamely onto his good foot. Brynn slung his arm around her shoulder and steadied him as he hopped to her car where she helped him into the front seat.

"I'll bring him right back," she called. "See you soon."

Jodie found herself alone with Jeff. His face knotted with worry as he watched Brynn drive away.

"He'll be okay," Jodie assured him.

Jeff nodded. "Gofer's a good man. He gave up joining a lucrative practice to work here. I hate to see him injured on top of his other sacrifices."

Jeff's concern was genuine, and for an instant Jodie fantasized what having Jeff care for her that deeply would feel like. The former Marine towered beside her, arms and chest bare where he'd stripped off his sweater in the afternoon sun to expose tanned muscles that sent her hormones into chaos. She tried to focus instead on the tattoo on his biceps, the Marine Corps

emblem emblazoned with *Semper Fi*. But his tantalizing smell distracted her. So much for deodorant
ads, she thought in desperation. Sweaty with his hair
flecked with sawdust, he probably hadn't a clue that
his masculine scent was driving her wild.

Time to deliver herself from temptation. Besides,
Brynn had left Brittany alone in the woods with Daniel, a situation that raised the hair on the back of Jodie's neck.

"I'll find Brittany." She silently cursed the breathlessness in her voice. "And we'll be going. I'll leave
the leftovers. There's probably enough for supper, at
least for your team."

Jeff gazed down at her, his gray eyes exuding a
warmth that sent her already giddy senses whirling.
"I can't thank you enough for today."

Jodie thought of a hundred ways he could thank
her, most of them deliciously indecent, and more heat
scorched her. She was probably red as a beet and
looked like an idiot. "You don't have to thank me.
You paid well."

He grinned. "I did, didn't I? But you were worth
every penny."

She wasn't about to ask him to elaborate. "I'm
glad the food met with your approval."

His expression sobered. "Some folks in town
won't approve of your being here. You took a risk,
catering for me. And I'm grateful."

The old Jeff, the ostracized teenager who had on

rare occasions dropped his don't-give-a-damn attitude to reveal his loneliness, peeked through the tough Marine demeanor, then disappeared so quickly, she thought she'd imagined his outcast look.

"I don't let other folks influence my decisions." She wished she could say the same for her hormones.

"I'll return your coolers and equipment tomorrow," he offered.

"Don't bother." She practically tripped over her tongue in her haste to reply. "Grant can pick up everything next time he checks your livestock. That'll save you a trip."

Jeff considered her, as if trying to discern her motives, and she looked toward the building site to avoid his scrutiny.

"I don't want to keep you from your work, so I'll get Brittany and we'll be going."

Before he could reply, she sprinted toward the footpath in the woods. Brittany had mentioned a creek, and Jodie seriously contemplated a dip in its icy waters to cool her blood and clear her head.

Chapter Four

In the bride's parlor of the Pleasant Valley Community Church, Jodie set aside her bridesmaid's bouquet of pale-pink roses and baby's breath, adjusted Merrilee Stratton's triple-tiered veil and smoothed a strand of pale-blond hair that had escaped from her friend's French twist.

"You look gorgeous," Jodie said. "There's nothing prettier than a June bride. Are you nervous?"

Merrilee shook her head and adjusted the pearl-encrusted neckline of her satin gown. Excitement sparkled in her sky-blue eyes.

"No second thoughts?" Jodie asked.

"I've never been more sure of anything in my entire life. That's how long I've loved your brother."

With her stiletto-heeled sandals killing her feet, Jodie sank onto the sofa, careful not to wrinkle the long skirt of her periwinkle-blue satin dress, and pondered how life was full of surprises. Six years ago, Merrilee had moved to New York to pursue her career in photography, and Jodie thought she'd lost her friend to the big city for good. Who would have guessed that Merrilee's parents, poster couple for happily marrieds, would separate, bringing Merrilee home on the first plane out of New York last March?

And who would have guessed that, in a few short months, Merrilee would reunite her parents, sell a photographic book on country vets to a major publisher and decide to follow her career in Pleasant Valley as Grant's wife?

"I've always wanted a sister," Jodie said.

"We've been like sisters since we were kids. My marrying Grant only makes it official."

Cat Stratton, Merrilee's mother, wearing an elegant designer dress in rose-colored silk that matched her cheeks, breezed through the door. The older woman, Jodie's high school English teacher and lifelong neighbor, had never looked happier. Evidently, her husband's midlife crisis had passed, and marital bliss had returned to the Stratton home.

"Wow, Mrs. Stratton," Jodie said, "you're a knockout in that dress."

"Thank you, dear. And look at the two of you. Who would ever have thought that the little girls who made mud pies in my backyard would turn into such beauties." Cat's eyes brimmed with joyful tears.

"Thanks, Mrs. S." To give mother and daughter a private moment, Jodie stood. "I'd better check on Brittany."

Jodie slipped out the door, wandered into the meditation garden and headed for a redwood bench beneath a crepe myrtle heavy with bright-pink blooms. Making it through the wedding and reception before her shoes killed her was going to take a miracle.

At least she didn't have to worry about running into Jeff Davidson. Grant had invited Jeff and his team to the wedding, but Archer Farm would open officially on Monday. And Jeff had admitted to Grant that, although the new building was almost finished, he had a punch list the size of a book to complete. Jeff, stripped to the waist, muscles rippling, his entrancing gray eyes concentrating on his task, was probably wielding a hammer or a paintbrush now, up to his very broad shoulders in last-minute details. And too far away, thank goodness, to distract Jodie from enjoying the wedding of her brother and her best friend.

Jodie closed her mind to the enticing picture of the bare-chested Marine. Jeff's absence suited her just fine. She had succeeded in avoiding him the last four weeks, in spite of his efforts to make contact. She'd had one of her staff or her voice mail field his numerous calls. And she'd slipped upstairs when he'd come into the café looking for her. Even the morning he'd brought his entire team for breakfast. So far she'd eluded him completely.

Except in her thoughts.

And her dreams.

As hard as she tried, Jodie couldn't scrub the man

from her mind, which was all the more reason to keep her distance. Arrogant young Randy Mercer had taught her an indelible lesson. Attractive men who sent her brain into shutdown mode were trouble with a capital *T*.

Add her reluctance to have Brittany involved with Daniel or Archer Farm's other delinquents, soon to arrive, and Jodie had the best of reasons to avoid Jeff Davidson like the plague.

"You ready, Mom?"

Jodie glanced up and had to look twice to recognize Brittany. Merrilee's wedding planner had flown in a hair stylist and makeup artist from New York for the women in the wedding party. The professionals had worked a miracle with Brittany. Gone was the sullen, ghostly teen with black-rimmed eyes. In her place stood a sophisticated young lady, blond hair in a flattering French braid, makeup understated to emphasize her youthful complexion, and on her nails—hallelujah!—pearly pink polish. The pastel of her blue dress brought out the creaminess of her skin. And not a speck of gloomy black in sight.

"You're beautiful, cupcake." Determined not to cry, Jodie blinked back tears.

"You really think so?"

"Turn around. Let me see all of you."

"Turn around? You've got to be kidding! I'll break my neck in these shoes!"

"Feet hurt?" Jodie asked.

"Oh, yeah," Brittany said with a grimace.

Jodie pushed to her aching feet. "You know what Gran Nathan always says."

"Pride knows no pain," mother and daughter said in unison and shared a grin.

"You watch," Brittany added. "I'll bet next week's allowance that Gran is wearing sensible shoes."

"I'm not biting. That's one bet I'd lose."

Jodie thought of her practical mother, who'd been a rock throughout Jodie's pregnancy and Brittany's early years. Jodie wouldn't have survived without her mother's unswerving love and support. Yes, Sophie Nathan would choose classy but comfortable shoes for her son's wedding, and she'd wear them with panache.

Brynn joined them, wearing the same style dress and shoes as Brittany and Jodie. Her statuesque posture and luscious curves, however, gave her satin gown an entirely different interpretation. Officer Sawyer, Jodie thought, without a smidgen of envy, would make a burlap sack look like haute couture.

"Merrilee and her dad are waiting at the front of the church," Brynn said. "It's show time."

As fast as their high-heeled sandals allowed, the bridesmaids hurried to the church's entrance. Cat Stratton walked down the aisle on the arm of a groomsman, one of Grant's friends from veterinary school.

"You're next." The wedding planner adjusted Brittany's bouquet and pushed her gently through the door.

A moment later Brynn stepped into the church. After the proper interval, Jodie trailed Brynn down the aisle. Focusing on the instructions from last night's rehearsal, Jodie was barely aware of the crowd that packed the sanctuary. Brittany had already arrived at the flower-decked chancel ablaze with branched candelabra. Brynn joined Brit, and finally Jodie reached the front of the church and turned to await the bride.

Next to the minister, Grant and her father, serving as best man, looked especially handsome in their tuxedos. They also eyed the back of the church.

Organ music swelled and filled the room, no ordinary wedding march for the artistic Merrilee, but a spectacular trumpet voluntary that raised goose flesh on the back of Jodie's neck. Merrilee appeared on her father's arm, and the entire congregation rose to their feet.

Jodie couldn't take her eyes off her best friend, who'd never looked more radiantly blissful. Not until Merrilee and Dr. Stratton reached the chancel and stood beside Grant did Jodie allow herself a glimpse of the packed congregation.

Her breath caught in her chest when her gaze swept the fifth pew on the groom's side. Standing literally head and shoulders above the others, dark suits immaculate, white shirts crisp and ties expertly knotted, were Jeff Davidson, his team and Daniel.

The Marines had landed.

IN THE SPACIOUS REAR GARDEN of the Victorian home of Sally Mae McDonough, Merrilee's formidable maternal grandmother, Jeff did a quick reconnaissance. Over half the town of Pleasant Valley had attended the wedding and proceeded to Mrs. McDonough's for the reception. Guests jammed the broad terraces and strolled the brick pathways, lighted by strands of tiny white lights and awash in the perfume of flowering confederate jasmine.

From his concealed vantage point in the gazebo at the back of the property, Jeff watched his team and young Daniel pay their respects to the bride and groom before making a quick but dignified retreat.

Weddings were definitely not a guy thing, but his buddies had been adamant about attending. Grant Nathan, the groom, and father-of-the-bride, Jim Stratton, had not only provided free veterinary care for Archer Farm's animals, the vets had also volunteered several Saturdays to work on the dorm building. His team was hastening back to the mountain now to handle last-minute details, but Jeff had ridden his Harley to town and would return later. He wasn't leaving until he'd completed his objective. Time was running out. He had to talk to Jodie.

As if his wish had conjured her, he caught sight of

a splash of sky-blue perfection as she wound her way through the guests toward the back of the garden. He drew behind the thick wisteria that covered the gazebo. He hadn't needed the skills of a re-con Marine to figure out that Jodie had been avoiding him the past four weeks. Or to know that, if she glimpsed him now, she'd run the other way.

She'd seemed open and friendly the day of the dorm raising. But afterward, she might as well have tattooed Keep Away, Jeff, across her forehead. Frustrated by his inability to make contact, Jeff had consulted his resident psychologist.

"Give it to me straight, Gofer. Did I do something to offend her?"

"Not that I observed. I think she likes you. Too much."

"What the hell is that supposed to mean?"

"You scare her."

"I never touched the woman!"

"I could be wrong, but—"

"No buts about it," Jeff had insisted. "Jodie's not scared. She's simply put off by my reputation. No Pleasant Valley woman in her right mind wants anything to do with me."

"You were that bad?" Amusement glistened in Gofer's pale-blue eyes. "What'd you do? Break their hearts?"

"Worse. I was the one their mothers warned them

about. The ultimate bad boy no girl would date. I never had a chance to break anyone's heart.''

"And that's what you want now? A chance to break Jodie's heart?''

Jeff scrubbed a hand across his chin. "I didn't ask to be analyzed, Gofer. All I want is advice. I need her help if Archer Farm is going to make it.''

Gofer's expression sobered. "She has a teenager, who, from the way the girl acts and dresses, is waging a major adolescent rebellion. Jodie may fear Archer Farm will be a negative influence on her daughter.''

"My business is with Jodie, not her daughter.''

Gofer crossed his thick arms across his powerful chest and leaned back in his desk chair. "You don't get it.''

Jeff drew a blank. "What?''

"Jodie and Brittany are a family. A package. What affects one affects the other. If you want Jodie's co-operation, you have to convince her that Archer Farm is no threat to her daughter.''

"No problem,'' Jeff insisted.

"Oh, you have a problem, all right. In case you haven't noticed, Daniel's been suffering from a major case of puppy love since he first laid eyes on Brittany.''

"You're sure?''

"It's my job to notice those things.''

"Brittany lives on the other end of the valley. And Daniel has no wheels.''

"Did that ever stop you?"

Jeff conceded the point. By the time he was eleven, he'd finessed the fine art of hitchhiking.

"Besides," Gofer continued, "integrating our kids into the community will be a major part of their rehabilitation. You know that."

Jeff sighed with frustration. "So how do I get Jodie's help?"

Gofer grinned. "Go for broke."

"Kidnap her?"

His friend shook his head. "Be honest. Just ask her."

"For advice like that," Jeff said with a wry grin, "I'm glad I'm not paying you by the hour."

Ask her, Gofer had said. Yeah, right. Jeff had to catch her first. Through a gap in the vines he observed Jodie's progress through the throng of guests. She was definitely headed his way.

Waiting for her to arrive, he scanned the party. Mrs. McDonough and the Strattons had spared no expense for Merrilee's reception. A full orchestra, seated beneath a muscadine arbor near the house, played the opening strains of a Broadway tune. Guests temporarily abandoned the buffet tables, laden with enough food to feed a Marine Corps brigade and three bottomless silver bowls of mint julep. Circling the lower terrace, they watched Merrilee dance with her father, then with Grant. Gloria, the wolfhound Grant had rescued months ago from the side of the

road, had been groomed for the occasion and be-
decked with a collar of pink roses and a blue bow
that matched the bridesmaids' dresses. Woofing happily, the dog orbited the bridal pair in her own canine
version of a waltz.

Jeff couldn't help grinning. Grant, in spite of his
monkey suit and all the ceremonious hoopla, looked
happy as a pig in mud. And the glance the newlyweds
exchanged threatened to accomplish what the warm
June evening hadn't—turn the ice sculptures to pud-
dles on the buffet tables.

Jodie reached the gazebo. She paused at the bottom
step, and Jeff held his breath. Glancing over her
shoulder, as if to make certain she was unobserved,
she slipped off her shoes. Barefoot, she hitched her
skirt with one hand, held her shoes in the other and
scampered up the stairs. Sinking onto the bench that
circled the wall, she exhaled what sounded like a sigh
of relief.

"Escaping?" Jeff asked from the shadows.

She flinched in surprise. "I didn't know anyone
was here." Her eyebrows drew together in a frown
that did nothing to mar her beauty. "Are you following me?"

"I was here first."

Flinging her arms along the back of the bench, she
stretched her feet in front of her and wiggled her toes.
Moonlight streamed through the wisteria and the gazebo's gingerbread trim, sparking iridescent high-

lights in her upswept hair and painting her bare arms and shoulders with a silvery sheen. She looked like a fairy princess he'd seen in a picture book when he'd been a child.

Then she spoke, and her caustic tone broke the spell. "I thought you weren't coming to the wedding."

"Changed my mind."

"Your dorm's finished?"

"No."

"Then why are you here?"

"To talk to you."

"I don't want to talk to you."

"Why not?"

His question seemed to stump her, because she didn't answer.

"I'm not asking for any special favors." He pressed his advantage while he had his opportunity. "Just a chance to offer a business deal."

"Tourist season's in full swing. I don't have time for catering." Her answer came instantly, without hesitation. She held her chin high and concentrated on the opposite side of the gazebo, avoiding his eyes.

"I don't want catering."

"What do you want?" she said sharply.

I want you.

God, where had that thought come from? He couldn't blame it on the mint julep. After watching his father's lifelong decline into alcoholism, Jeff had never touched a drop of liquor of any kind, fearful that the same genetic components that had doomed his father would snare him in their grip.

"You run a restaurant and gift shop," Jeff began.

"Well, there's a news flash."

Jodie's sarcasm wasn't making his task any easier. While he struggled for the right words, she pushed to her feet, winced in obvious pain, and sat again.

He nodded toward the shoes in her hand. "Feet hurt?"

She started to stand again, but Jeff hadn't lost his finely honed Marine reflexes. Before her attractive behind left the bench, he was on his knees with her feet in his hands. She tried to pull away, but he gripped her gently. The softness of her warm, bare flesh shot spirals of pleasure through him.

Concentrate, jarhead. Don't let her get away.

"I'm very familiar with aching feet. Occupational hazard," he said breezily while his fingers expertly massaged her arches and toes. "They say an army moves on its stomach. Funny thing, my stomach never hurt after a thirty-mile forced march. Only my feet."

She leaned her head against the gazebo railing and moaned softly. "Feels wonderful. Where did you learn that?"

"Kermit. His mother is a massage therapist."

"I think you've saved my life. I should be out there

with Grant and Merrilee, but I couldn't stay on my feet a minute longer.''

"Go barefoot. As much mint julep as everyone's consumed, who'd notice?''

"Mrs. McDonough, for one. She's a stickler for propriety.'' Jodie pulled her feet from his hands. "I have to go.''

Jodie leaned over to put on her shoes, her face mere inches from his. Her warm breath fanned his cheek, her light magnolia fragrance enveloped him, and her strapless gown revealed a tantalizing glimpse of cleavage. She quickly slipped on her shoes, and her fingers fumbled with his as she fastened the straps.

Later, when he attempted to analyze what had happened next, he'd tried to blame the flower-scented summer night air, the romantic melody the orchestra had played and the fact he'd been apart from women for so long. But in the end, he'd reached only one conclusion. He'd kissed her because he'd wanted to, more than anything, even more than asking for her help with Archer Farm.

And he'd caught her totally by surprise. Cradling her face between his callused palms, he pulled her to him and covered her lips with his. She tasted of sweetness and innocence and untapped passion. Reason clanged a warning, ordered him to stop, to consider the consequences, but he couldn't. Not while she was kissing him back, blowing common sense to kingdom come.

He stood, drew her to him, and slid his arms around her. Her body melted into his, her arms circled his neck and the kiss deepened. The soft curve of her breasts met the hardness of his chest, and the pounding of her heart matched his own beat.

Suddenly she stiffened, placed her hands against his chest, and pushed him away.

"Red light, Marine," she snapped like an order.

Red light? How in hell did Jodie know the military warning for sexual harassment? And even worse, was that all his kiss had meant to her?

He stepped away instantly, labored to control his breathing and noted with satisfaction that she seemed as rattled by the kiss as he was. The rosy pink of her face glowed, even in the faint moonlight.

"Was that your idea of talking?" She rubbed the tips of her fingers across her lips as if trying to erase his touch.

He stifled a groan. "No."

Straightening her shoulders, she crossed her arms over her chest and glared. "What, no apology?"

How could he say he was sorry when he wasn't? Kissing Jodie ranked right up there as one of the top five experiences of his life. He was saved from answering by Brynn Sawyer's entry into the gazebo.

"Jodie, thank God. I've been looking all over for you. Grant and Merrilee are ready to leave." With barely a glance at Jeff, Brynn hurried away.

Jodie started to follow.

"Wait, please," Jeff begged.

"I have to go."

"Tell me when we can talk."

Jodie hastened across the gazebo and threw her parting words over her shoulder. "When hell freezes over."

Chapter Five

Jodie squinted in the bright afternoon sunshine and climbed the stairs of Mrs. Weatherstone's impressive three-story Victorian a block off Piedmont Avenue, the town's main street where her café was located.

Four-o'clock tea with the delightful octogenarian wasn't exactly Jodie's Sunday activity of choice. Up late last night at the reception, awake before dawn to prepare for the weekend breakfast crowd and suffering terminal embarrassment after her shameless encounter with Jeff in the gazebo, all Jodie wanted was to climb into bed, pull the covers over her head and sleep. Preferably until Brittany turned forty.

But in addition to being fond of sweet Mrs. Weatherstone, Jodie also owed the elderly woman. Big time. Seven years ago, Mrs. Weatherstone had sold Jodie the downtown building for her Mountain Crafts and Café. Sold it, Jodie thought with a laugh. The old darling had practically given her the place at an outrageously low asking price. Without Mrs. Weatherstone's generosity, Jodie wouldn't be self-reliant to-day. So when the elderly woman had called midmorning and invited Jodie to afternoon tea to fill her in on Grant and Merrilee's wedding, Jodie couldn't refuse.

Her face heated from more than the June sun when she remembered the previous night. She'd not only kissed Jeff with abandon, she'd enjoyed kissing him. Enjoyed it too much. And the excitement had scared the daylights out of her. She'd been rude as a result. But she'd also been resolute. She would not speak with him again. Ever. As far as she was concerned, she and Jeff had nothing to talk about.

A groan escaped at the memory of her stupid "red light" warning. She might as well have admitted outright that she'd spent too many evenings the past eight years watching reruns of *JAG,* a glaring testament to the fact that, beyond her business and Brittany, she didn't have a life.

After her hasty exit from the gazebo, she'd joined the other guests at the front curb to cheer Grant and Merrilee's departure for their honeymoon. And she'd been mortified when Merrilee tossed the bridal bouquet of white roses and stephanotis directly into her hands. The irony of a never-married woman with a fourteen-year-old destined to become the next bride had hit Jodie hard. And the scorching look from Jeff, standing across the street beside his Harley, had registered even harder.

Shoving away the memory of the searing scrutiny in those thundercloud-gray eyes, Jodie stepped into the cooling shade of the broad porch, approached the massive double doors with stained-glass panels and rang the bell. The door opened almost immediately.

"I'm delighted to see you, Jodie, dear," Mrs. Weatherstone greeted her.

The tiny woman with birdlike bones was, as always, fastidiously dressed, today in a lavender summer dress of cotton voile with her trademark string of pearls and a pair of sturdy white brogans. Soft white hair framed her face, lined with age, and accented her violet eyes.

"Come in out of the heat. Tea's almost ready." She pivoted her metal walker and led the way down the wide hallway into the front parlor, trailing a faint scent of lilacs behind her.

Jodie followed into a room filled with heavy antiques and bright with sunlight. Jim Dandy, Mrs. Weatherstone's chihuahua, lay on a love seat in a puddle of sunshine streaming through one of the tall windows. At the sound of footsteps, the dog lifted its head, regarded Jodie with huge brown eyes and, recognizing no threat, went back to sleep.

Mrs. Weatherstone sat beside Jim Dandy, caressed his tiny head with an arthritic hand and motioned Jodie to the love seat opposite her. "Lunch was especially delicious today, dear. My compliments to Maria, your wonderful cook, and my gratitude to you."

Ever since Jodie had opened her café, she'd had lunch delivered everyday to Mrs. Weatherstone. At first the older woman had protested, but Jodie had insisted. The meals-on-wheels were a thank-you for enabling her to purchase the building, and, as Mrs. Weatherstone grew frailer each year, the hearty lunches helped her to remain independent in the home she loved so dearly.

A refrigerator door slammed in the large kitchen at the back of the house, and Jodie guessed her hostess had hired a local teenager to prepare tea. Mrs. Weatherstone claimed having teens around kept her young. She'd even paid Brittany on occasion for light housekeeping and weeding her flower beds.

"Now." Her hostess rubbed her hands together, and her violet eyes sparkled with anticipation. "Tell me all about the wedding. I regret that these old bones prevented my attendance."

Jodie launched into a description of Merrilee and the rest of the wedding party, the flowers, the music, the guests and Mrs. McDonough's elaborate reception.

When she mentioned Gloria with her special floral collar, Mrs. Weatherstone gasped. "Grant actually took that wolfhound to the wedding?"

"Grant's worked miracles with her. She doesn't tear things up now and she's very obedient. Gloria sat next to Grant and Daddy through the entire ceremony in the church and didn't make a sound. But her tail-wagging almost knocked over an eight-branched candelabra.''

''And she performed her own version of the wedding waltz,'' a familiar male voice chimed in.

Jeff, holding a tray of iced tea and cookies, stood in the arched doorway. Dressed in black trousers with a gray knit shirt, he looked even more mouthwatering than he had in his suit last night.

When he'd kissed her. In a way she'd never been kissed before.

Heat swept through Jodie at the memory.

''What are you doing here?'' She regretted the bluntness of her question immediately, but Jeff had caught her by surprise. To her knowledge, Jeff didn't even know Mrs. Weatherstone. He'd never had much contact with any of the people who lived in town.

''Why, he's having tea with us, dear,'' Mrs. Weatherstone said matter-of-factly, as if Pleasant Valley's notorious bad boy's presence in her living room was a customary occurrence. ''Put the tray on the coffee table, please, Jeff, and sit by me.''

''You two know each other?'' Jodie felt as dazed as the time a yellow jacket had stung her right between the eyes. This house was the last place she'd expected to find Jeff Davidson.

Mrs. Weatherstone accepted the glass of iced tea Jeff offered and smiled up at him. ''Jeff and I are good friends.''

Jodie's brain whirled. What in the world did Mrs. Weatherstone have in common with Jeff?

Jeff handed Jodie a glass of tea and offered a plate of home-baked cookies. She accepted the glass and took a cookie automatically, her mind still trying to assimilate the puzzle before her.

She stared at the cookie in surprise. "You made these, Mrs. Weatherstone?"

The elderly woman barely managed to prepare her own breakfast and a simple supper. She definitely lacked the stamina for baking. Maybe a neighbor had brought them.

Jeff selected a glass of tea and a cookie for himself and folded his large frame onto the love seat next to Jim Dandy. "Trace baked the cookies."

"Trace?" Jodie was feeling more and more like Alice who'd just fallen down the rabbit hole.

"Lovely boys, Jeff's Marines," Mrs. Weatherstone said with a nod.

"We've divided duties at the farm." Jeff sneaked a piece of cookie to the dog. "Gofer's our psychologist. Trace does the cooking."

"And a good job, too," the older woman said. "These cookies are delicious."

"Kermit's in charge of the animals, and Ricochet takes care of the gardens."

Since Jodie couldn't rush out immediately without upsetting Mrs. Weatherstone, she opted for polite conversation until she could make her escape. "What's your job?"

"Administration and fund-raising," Jeff said.

Fund-raising.

Suspicion raised its ugly head. Mrs. Weatherstone had a large fortune, inherited from her father, who'd made millions in textiles after World War II. Was Jeff after the old lady's money to finance Archer Farm?

Mrs. Weatherstone set her iced tea aside and grabbed her walker to hoist herself to her feet. "If you young people will excuse me, I'm going to powder my nose."

Jeff stood at the same time.

"You can tell Jodie all about us while I'm gone," Mrs. Weatherstone said.

Jodie waited until Mrs. Weatherstone had moved out of earshot down the hall before jumping to her feet and turning on him. "Of all the sneaking, lowdown, conniving tricks! How dare you manipulate that sweet old lady?"

Jeff's expression darkened with an anger so fierce that Jodie took a step back.

"Mrs. Weatherstone is a saint," he said. "I'd never take advantage of her."

"Looks like you just did, buster, using her to get to me."

Jodie wanted to bolt for the door, but Jeff stood in her way, as big and impassable as the rock face of Devil's Mountain. If her anger rattled him, he didn't show it. Cool, imperturbable and handsome as sin. That pretty much summed him up.

"Tell her I had a headache," Jodie said, "and had to leave."

"You want me to lie for you?" He arched an eyebrow and skewered her with a gray-eyed glance that made her knees weak.

She had to escape before she did something stupid, like throwing herself against that solid chest and kissing him again. She breathed deeply to block the emotion from her voice. "I don't want to hurt her feelings. Mrs. Weatherstone's been good to me."

"Me, too. Want to hear how?"

"No." She started around him.

He moved into her path. "You're really not interested?"

"Why should I be?"

"You live in Pleasant Valley. Everybody here has an insatiable hunger to know everyone else's business."

"I never pay attention to small-town gossip."

"We have that in common," he said reasonably, "and Mrs. Weatherstone."

Jodie had to get away before her rebellious senses hijacked her reason and encouraged her to repeat last night's mistakes. "You won't let me leave?"

Jeff stepped aside. "You can go anytime. But Mrs. Weatherstone wants you to help me. That's why she invited you today. If you're turning me down, you can tell her yourself. I'll go get her.''

"Wait!" Jodie loved Mrs. Weatherstone like a grandmother and couldn't bear the thought of disappointing her. How could Jodie tell the older woman she'd refused to help Jeff when she hadn't even listened to what he wanted?

"I'm waiting," Jeff said mildly, obviously enjoying the upper hand.

Jodie conceded defeat. "I'll hear what you have to say, but I'm not making any promises."

"Fair enough." He nodded solemnly.

"And there have to be ground rules."

"Ground rules?" Amusement tugged at the corners of his very kissable mouth.

She jerked her gaze away, concentrated on the sleeping dog and backed onto the love seat. "No touching."

"No touching," he agreed.

She didn't look at his face, but she could hear the laughter in his voice. "And that includes kissing," she emphasized.

"You didn't like our kiss?" He sounded surprised.

Jodie took a deep breath. "Whether I liked it or not is irrelevant."

"You accused me of sexual harassment. That was a low blow."

"Do you always go around kissing women who don't want to be kissed?"

"I'm sorry if I misinterpreted your wishes," he said with apparent sincerity. "I'll obey your ground rules if you'll listen to my proposal."

Jodie took a swallow of iced tea to douse the warmth consuming her. She wouldn't accept Jeff's proposition, no matter what it was, but she had to know about his relationship to Mrs. Weatherstone. If he was working a con on the old lady, Jodie intended to put a stop to it.

"Mrs. Weatherstone said to tell me about the two of you," she reminded him. "I want to hear that first."

Jeff pulled a chair close to the love seat and sat. Jodie realized she should have extended her ground rules to include keeping his distance. Although he wasn't actually touching her, as he'd promised, his proximity was distracting. He smelled of clothes fresh from the dryer, sunshine and a distinctive masculine scent that teased her senses. She took another cooling drink of tea and avoided his auger-like gaze.

"Mrs. Weatherstone came into my life twenty-nine years ago," he began.

Jeff was Grant's age. Jodie did a quick calculation, and the results astonished her. "You were only five."

He nodded. "I was in kindergarten at Pleasant Valley Elementary. Mrs. Weatherstone volunteered as a mentor, and I was lucky enough to be assigned to her."

"She helped with your schoolwork?"

"She saved my life." The words, spoken so quietly and with such conviction, echoed in the room.

"I don't understand." Jodie could no longer avoid looking at him. His eyes were dark with memory, the strong angles of his face softened by affection.

"My mother died shortly after I was born, and I was sent to live with an aunt in North Carolina. She had too little money and too many of her own children, so as soon as I was school age, she packed me up and brought me back to my father. He wasn't home that day, and she left me alone on the front porch to wait."

Jodie pictured a lonely little boy, abandoned at the unfamiliar mountain farm by the only family he'd ever known. Her heart went out to him, in spite of her determination to remain aloof.

"Daddy enrolled me in preschool," Jeff continued. "Not that he was a great believer in education. I was too little to work, and he wanted me out of his hair."

Jodie couldn't imagine the pain of the young boy's situation: no mother and a father who didn't want him. How had he survived?

"The day I met Mrs. Weatherstone who was mentoring in my kindergarten class," Jeff continued in a voice that betrayed none of his feelings, "it was mid-December, twenty-three degrees and snowing. I had only a thin jacket that was too small and shoes with the soles half-gone."

The image of the cold little boy wrung Jodie's

heart. "I'm surprised Child Welfare didn't place you in a foster home."

"They tried. Daddy greeted the social workers with a shotgun. Warned he'd blow them all to hell if they set foot on his property again. He was paranoid, believed all governmental agencies were in cahoots, and feared they'd discover his still. Chief Sawyer tried to talk to him, but Daddy said they'd have to take him to court to get me, and to do that, they'd have to catch him first. That was the last I ever saw of Social Services.

"Not long after, I encountered Mrs. Weatherstone at school. When she realized I had no money and no food, she brought me here during the lunch hour and fed me, not only that first day but every school day until I graduated high school. That day she also bought me shoes, boots, a warm coat with a hood and mittens. She upgraded my wardrobe as needed to keep up with my growth spurts. And she always sent me home on Friday with enough food for the weekend. It would have been enough, if Daddy hadn't eaten most of it."

Jodie shivered with revulsion. Hiram Davidson must have been a monster, stealing food from his own child. "Living with him must have been hard."

Jeff shrugged. "It was the only life I knew. I didn't realize until I was a few years older that all fathers weren't like him. Mr. Weatherstone was still alive then, and he was more a father to me than mine ever was. He'd take me to his shop, where your café is now, and teach me to fix things. When I entered high school, he bought the Harley I have now. It was a piece of rolling junk, but we restored it together.''

Doubt gnawed at her, and Jodie narrowed her eyes. ''I didn't know any of this, and, as you say, everyone in Pleasant Valley knows everything about each other.''

''The Weatherstones kept their interest in me a secret, for my sake. They knew my father's hot temper and possessive attitude. He wouldn't take care of me, but he didn't want anyone else butting into his business, either. He'd have locked me up and forbidden me to see the Weatherstones if he'd known.''

Jodie couldn't help thinking of her own dad, big and jovial, always ready with a hug and unconditional love. Even when she'd embarrassed him by becoming pregnant as a teen, he'd never turned his back on her, never made her doubt for an instant that he cared more about her and Brittany than anyone else in the world. Including her mom and Grant, of course.

Jeff hadn't had a mom. And only a sorry excuse for a father. And now the former Marine was devoting his life to rescuing other kids whose situations were probably as desperate as his own had been. Jodie's attitude toward Archer Farm was softening, and she gave herself a mental shake. Not all down-and-out kids turned out as well as Jeff had. State and federal prisons were filled with people whose miserable childhood and/or bad company had set their feet on an irreversible path of crime and destruction.

"Once I reached junior high," Jeff said, "I told my father I was working for the Weatherstones. They paid me to care for the lawns and gardens, to sweep out Mr. Weatherstone's shop, to run errands on the Harley. Dad didn't complain, as long as I gave him the major part of my earnings."

"You must have hated him," Jodie said.

Jeff leaned forward, clasped his strong hands between his knees, and regarded her with a puzzled look. "I did, but I loved him, too. Or I loved the father I wanted him to be."

"And you joined the Marines to get away from him?"

"The Weatherstones offered to send me to college, but I knew I wouldn't fit in. I had no idea what I wanted to do with my life. I just wanted to get as far away from Pleasant Valley as I could."

"Why did you come back?"

"I hadn't planned to. As mean as my daddy was, I figured he'd live forever. Like in the old saying 'Only the good die young.'"

Jeff's face clouded, and Jodie guessed his sorrow was for his friend, Captain Archer, not his father.

"Arch and I had discussed buying land somewhere out west. But when my father died and the homestead became mine, we decided to locate here. With the land, house, barn and outbuildings in hand, our initial expenses dropped considerably.'' Jeff sighed. ''I didn't know then that money wouldn't be a major problem.''

Jodie's protective instincts raised the hackles on her the back of her neck. Had he cajoled Mrs. Weatherstone into bankrolling his farm? ''Why not?''

''Arch.'' Jeff's voice, controlled and steady when he'd spoken of his mother's death and his father's abuse, broke on his friend's name. He cleared his throat. ''Since we were both orphans, we named each other beneficiaries on our life insurance policies.''

''Oh.'' Jodie resisted the overwhelming urge to put her arms around him and comfort him.

''Ironic, isn't it?'' His expression held more pain than irony. ''Arch's dying helped make our dream come true.''

Jodie could tell, however, that Jeff would rather have his friend alive, even if it meant a hardscrabble life to support their project.

Your sympathy's kicking in, she warned herself, *along with your attraction. You'll find yourself in hot water if you're not careful.*

Time for a hasty retreat. Enough of the story of his life. She cut to the chase. ''You have your place and your funding, so why do you need me?''

Jeff cleared his throat again. When he spoke, the huskiness of loss was replaced by a strictly business tone. ''I invested the money from Arch's policy, but in today's economy, even with state and federal subsidy grants, the funds won't last forever. Archer Farm has to become self-sufficient.''

His words rocked her backward. "That's a tall order.''

"That's where you come in.''

"My business barely pays its way and supports Brittany and me.''

"That's why my plan will be good for both of us.''

She raised an eyebrow and regarded him with skepticism. "I'm listening.''

He leaned closer, his expression earnest with an appealing boyish quality. "Archer Farm will provide you with fresh herbs and vegetables, milk, eggs and even goat cheese, at below wholesale prices.''

The idea sounded good. Too good. "What's the catch?''

"You hire a few of my clients as busboys and dishwashers.''

"You've got to be kidding! I don't want to scare off my customers.''

"I'll vouch for my clients.'' His boyish grin widened. "And I'll keep close tabs on them. In addition to saving money on your food purchases, you'll have the help you need and my boys will learn the satisfaction of doing a job well and earning a paycheck.''

Jodie expelled a deep breath. Talk about putting the fox in the hen house. Not only would Jeff's delinquents be in constant contact with Brittany, but Jeff would be popping into the café on a regular basis to evaluate his charges.

"I don't know...." Jodie shook her head.

"There's more," Jeff said.

"More?" His proposal had already boggled her mind. What more could he ask?

"We intend to keep the teens busy."

"Idle hands are the devil's workshop." One of her mother's favorite sayings had sprung automatically to her lips.

He nodded. "They'll care for the animals, plant and maintain the gardens and perform housekeeping chores. But we want them to have a creative outlet, too."

"Something to replace stealing cars and shoplifting?" She hadn't even tried to throttle her sarcasm.

But apparently nothing she said could dampen his enthusiasm. "They'll learn mountain crafts, basket weaving, quilt making, even pottery."

In spite of her efforts to remain objective, she found his excitement contagious. "You've planned every detail, haven't you?"

"These kids need to learn self-respect and the satisfaction of hard work."

She sighed. "And I suppose you want me to sell their crafts in my gift shop?"

"At a fair commission, of course."

She couldn't agree to his plan, for a multitude of

reasons, all personal. But she had to give him credit for ingenuity.

"Don't make up your mind yet," Jeff said quickly, as if sensing that she was about to decline. "Take time to consider it."

"I think your helping Jeff is a wonderful idea." Mrs. Weatherstone leaned on her walker in the doorway. "You will give it some thought, won't you, Jodie?"

Jodie, caught between the proverbial rock and hard place, glanced from the older woman's smiling face to the pleading look in Jeff's eyes.

"Of course," she heard herself agreeing. "I'll give it some thought."

"I'm so glad," Mrs. Weatherstone said. "I knew I could count on you. After all, you and Jeff are two of my favorite people."

Jodie forced a smile. She'd consented only to considering Jeff's proposal. But what she actually had to think about was a way to turn him down without Mrs. Weatherstone's believing Jodie was a heartless ingrate.

Chapter Six

After driving back from Mrs. Weatherstone's, Jeff parked the Harley in front of the farmhouse, surveyed Archer Farm with a critical stare and tried to envision it through the eyes of the ten new clients who would arrive the next day.

His formerly ramshackle home glistened with a fresh coat of white paint, and new green shutters framed the sparkling-clean windows. The surrounding lawn was neatly trimmed, and the flowers Ricochet had planted were a burst of bright hues around the foundation of the porch.

Ricochet was working now in the garden, freshly tilled beside the newly completed dorm. He was taking advantage of the long summer day to set out the last of the tomato plants. He raised his head and waved before returning to his task. Jeff acknowledged him with a salute, turning to formality to fight off the lump in his throat. His team had bought into his dream, lock, stock and barrel, even at the ridiculously low pay that was all he could afford. His men were the reason Archer Farm was up and running, ready for tomorrow's arrivals. Without his men's help, the project would have taken years to launch.

Beyond the newly painted red barn on the other side of the farmhouse, young kids in the goat herd frolicked in the pasture above the pond. Kermit, visible through the open barn door, was completing the evening milking. Jeff inhaled a deep breath. Along with the scent of moist, rich earth and assorted livestock smells, the fragrances of spices and baking filled the summer breeze. Trace was probably slaving in the kitchen, preparing heat-and-serve dishes for the freezer for the busy days ahead.

Gofer sat in a rocking chair on the front porch, his work boots propped on the balustrade, his head bent over a case file folder. Jeff's gut tightened. Gofer's ability to counsel their clients would be critical to rehabilitating the boys who were depending on them.

Gofer's progress with Daniel was a good omen. Jeff spotted the teen on his knees in the garden, helping Ricochet with the planting. Over the past few weeks, the boy had lost his scared-rabbit demeanor. Daniel behaved more like an overgrown, friendly puppy now. He'd taken a particular shine to Ricochet, who didn't seem to mind being tailed constantly by the hero-worshipping teen.

Gofer glanced up as Jeff approached the porch. "Any luck with Plan B?"

Jeff sank onto the top step and leaned against a porch post. "Hard to tell. Jodie said she'd think about helping us."

"You don't sound encouraged."

"I'm not. The woman wants nothing to do with me or Archer Farm."

Damn, he shouldn't have kissed her at the reception. His presumption had angered her, made her throw up her defenses and man the barricades. But nothing a re-con Marine couldn't handle, he assured himself, and hoped he was right. He wanted her as an ally. A partner.

Most of all, he wanted to kiss her again.

Yeah, right. And she'd have him arrested for sexual harassment. He'd be a great example for his teenagers then.

Try as he might, he couldn't get her out of his mind. The pale-green dress she'd worn this afternoon had brought out the green in her hazel eyes and clung to her soft curves like his Harley hugged the road. And her sandals had exposed delectable toes with pale-pink polish on the nails. He remembered the warmth of her feet in his hands in the gazebo—

Forget her charms and concentrate on business, he ordered himself. *Tomorrow, counting Daniel, you'll be responsible for eleven teenage boys. The last thing you need is a woman complicating your life and distracting you from your goals.*

Gofer dropped his feet to the floor and leaned toward him. "Your friend Mrs. Weatherstone couldn't persuade her?"

Jeff shook his head. "She tried."

"So what's Plan C?"

"Contact some restaurants and shops in Walhalla and Cashiers. Offer them the same deal."

The telephone rang inside the farmhouse.

"So," Gofer said with a reassuring grin, "you still have options."

"Yeah." But not the option he wanted.

Trace opened the screen door. "Phone's for you, Jeff. It's Jodie Nathan."

Gofer raised his eyebrows. "Suppose she's changed her mind?"

"Has hell frozen over?" Jeff pushed to his feet. "My guess is she's thought about my offer and is calling to give me a definite no."

With a sinking feeling, he followed Trace into the house. What did it matter if Jodie turned him down? They barely knew each other.

That's why it mattered, he realized with a jolt. Jodie interested him more than any woman he'd ever met, and he wanted to know her a whole lot better.

Fat chance.

Trace returned to the kitchen, and Jeff stopped at the hall table and picked up the receiver.

"It's Jodie," she said with a hint of breathlessness when he answered. "I've decided to accept your busi-

ness offer. Can we meet at the farm tomorrow afternoon to discuss terms?''

He held the phone at arm's length and stared as if
it had bitten him before replacing it to his ear. ''Yes,
but—''

''Two o'clock,'' she said in a brisk, no-nonsense
tone. ''See you then.''

The line went dead.

Shell-shocked, Jeff sank into the nearest chair.
He'd traveled the world, studied different cultures,
mastered battle and reconnaissance tactics, and had
recently taken crash courses in business administration, agriculture, animal husbandry and adolescent
psychology. But he didn't know a damned thing about
women.

Especially a woman like Jodie.

His mouth stretched into a slow grin. Now, however, he might have a chance to find out.

''I CAN'T BELIEVE I'm doing exactly what that infu-
riating man asked.'' Jodie eased off the accelerator
until the van slowed below the speed limit. She didn't
want to arrive early at Archer Farm and appear too
eager. ''And I'm also talking to myself, a sure sign
that I've totally lost my mind.''

When she had left Mrs. Weatherstone's yesterday,
thoroughly convinced that wild horses couldn't drag
her into a business arrangement with Jeff, she'd gone

straight to her mother's to pick up Brittany, who had spent the afternoon with her grandparents.

When Jodie arrived at the rambling, two-story house just a few blocks from Mrs. Weatherstone's, she found her daughter in the family room, watching a baseball game on TV with Jodie's father and painting her fingernails and toenails black again. Jodie sighed. So much for the brief respite from Brittany's Goth phase.

Leaving the pair to their game, Jodie wandered through the homey kitchen and out the door to the backyard. Her mother reclined in an Adirondack chair in the shade of an apple tree with her feet propped on a wooden footstool, a book open in her lap.

"Hi, darlin'," she called. "Come join me. Feet still hurt?"

Jodie sat in the chair usually reserved for her father and frowned. "They're the least of my problems."

"Better tell me about it." Sophie closed her book and gave Jodie her undivided attention. With dark hair and eyes like Grant, short and pleasantly plump, her mother reminded her of an energetic sparrow.

Jodie described her afternoon at Mrs. Weatherstone's and outlined Jeff's proposition. "But I can't have anything to do with him, Mama."

Sophie's eyes constricted in disappointment. "You haven't signed that petition?"

"What petition?"

"People were talking about it at the reception last

night. Some folks want the county to pass an ordinance banning Archer Farm's operation as a rehabilitation facility. They don't want all those troubled teens in the area.''

"That's not fair." The injustice offended her. "Jeff's put his heart and soul into this project." She thought for a moment. "On the other hand..."

"You agree with them?" Sophie looked surprised.

A persistent worry niggled at Jodie's brain, and she came clean, as always, with her mother. "I can relate to their fears because I'm concerned for Brittany, but I'd never try to shut down Archer Farm. I'll just keep her away from its residents."

Her mother tilted her head to one side and eyed Jodie with a bright-eyed, searching glance. "If you're not against the farm, why won't you take his business offer? It could increase your profits."

Jodie squirmed beneath her mother's scrutiny. "It's hard to explain."

"Are you falling in love with him?"

"No!" Jodie answered immediately but couldn't stop the flush that spread from her neck to her forehead.

"You're sure?"

Glad she could talk to Sophie about anything, Jodie answered, "My heart beats faster around him. My palms sweat and my knees go weak. And my brain shuts down completely, so that all I can think about is Jeff. But I felt the same way about Randy Mercer.

And once my head cleared, I knew I didn't love him."

Sophie nodded in agreement. "You were infatuated. That's not the same as love."

"I was a teenager then. I'm thirty years old now, but I feel fifteen all over again when Jeff walks through the door."

Her mother's pretty face with its rosy apple cheeks took on a musing cast. "Not all infatuations lead to love. But almost all love begins with infatuation."

"So how do you know when it's really love?" Jodie asked.

"First, you have to *like* the man."

Jodie scowled. "I like plenty of men, but I don't love them, at least not in a romantic way."

Sophie's eyes held a faraway look, as if she were remembering falling in love. "Physical thrills aren't enough. When you love someone, you want to wake up every morning to see his face on the pillow next to you. You can't wait to share everything that happens in your life and his, even the insignificant day-to-day details. And you place his happiness and well-being at the top of your priority list, right beside your own. Most of all, you can't imagine living in a world without him."

With a wave of relief, Jodie stood and paced the thick grass that her father tended so carefully. "So I can't love Jeff. I hardly know him. As far as I'm aware, we have nothing in common."

Sophie's smile was the sweetest Jodie had ever seen. "Getting to know someone can be a great cure for infatuation. Maybe you should spend more time with him. Get him out of your system, so to speak."

"He scares me, Mama."

"Does Jeff scare you, or are you afraid of yourself?" Sophie asked softly.

Jodie sank back into her chair. "I don't want to end up pregnant and abandoned again."

Her mother leaned over and patted her knee. "You're a different person from that shy, awkward teen that Randy Mercer took advantage of. You needn't worry. Besides, with the opposition brewing in this town, Jeff needs all the friends he can get. Grant insists Jeff's a good and decent man. And considering what he's doing at Archer Farm, his heart is certainly in the right place. Maybe you were too hasty in refusing his offer."

"From the sound of the campaign mounted against him, he'll need some friends," Jodie agreed. "Maybe with us, the Strattons and Mrs. Weatherstone as allies, he can beat this petition."

"Just remember, sometimes friendship turns into something more," her mother reminded her. "Your father's been my best friend for over thirty-seven years."

"And sometimes plain friendship is enough," Jodie said firmly.

She stood, put her arms around her mother and

noted that the gray had become more prevalent than brown in her thick hair. She kissed her mother's cheek. "Thanks, Mama. I love you."

"All things work to the good," Sophie reminded her and returned her hug.

Jodie had left her mother reading her book and gone into the house to call Jeff.

Today, however, she was second-guessing her decision and questioning her motives. Had she agreed with her mother because allying with Jeff was the right thing to do? Or had she been driven by the infatuation she was hoping to work out of her system? One fact was certain. Jodie wouldn't allow herself to make foolish mistakes. If Jeff's appeal threatened her reason, she'd remember her mother's calm, cool logic and keep her head on straight.

Buoyed by her internal pep talk, she pressed the gas pedal again.

When she arrived at the farm, however, the sight of Jeff, tanned and buff in cargo shorts, taut olive-drab T-shirt and work boots, blew all logic and reason to smithereens. Striding down the walk to meet her, he'd never looked more appealing. His wide, welcoming smile made her heart pound against her rib cage.

"What do you think of the place?" he asked with obvious pride. "Different from the last time you were here, huh?"

She dragged her attention from the handsome angles of his face and the well-developed muscles beneath the strained cotton of his shirt and looked around. Every building gleamed with fresh paint, flowers blossomed at each entry, even by the chicken coop, and the formerly stark red clay of the lawn and gardens sprouted young green growth.

"Wow. You guys are miracle workers," she said with awe. "You did all this in a month?"

"We had help. Grant and Dr. Stratton gave us a hand. Jay-Jay came up from his garage in town and tuned up Daddy's old tractor. Everything's coming together just in time. Our clients should arrive any minute. Let me give you the tour."

Jodie fell in step beside him and noted that he adjusted his long stride to match her shorter steps. He towered a foot above her, and she couldn't stop thinking of how those powerful arms had encircled her Saturday night in the gazebo, or how strong and solid his body had felt against hers. Even in the open air, his tantalizing scent led her thoughts in dangerous directions.

It's merely infatuation, a physical attraction, she reminded herself. *You'll get over it, so get a grip.*

They entered the new dorm first. What had been a skeleton of timbers when Jodie last saw it was now as inviting as a mountain lodge resort. A huge stone fireplace at one end of the great room had several deep leather sofas grouped in front. Large windows offered sweeping vistas of the surrounding mountains and the valley below. Braided rugs, plump cushions and matching draperies added splashes of color. Someone had filled pottery jugs with Queen Anne's lace and black-eyed Susans and placed them on the mantel and side tables for a cozy touch.

Opposite the great room, immaculate stainless steel commercial-grade appliances like the ones in her café dominated the kitchen. A huge dining table, big enough for twenty, doubled as a work station. Behind the kitchen, a hall opened onto four small bedrooms for the resident counselors with a private sitting room containing a media center and bookshelves, and two adjoining bathrooms.

"The team's been living in the house," Jeff said, "but they'll move in here tonight."

"None of them is married?" Jodie asked.

Jeff shook his head. "Re-con Marines don't make good husbands."

"Why not?" Maybe his answer would supply more reasons to resist him.

"They're deployed at a moment's notice," Jeff said, "and they can't say where they're going or when—or if—they'll return. Those conditions don't foster good family situations."

"But your team's not in the Marines any longer."

Jeff rolled back the sleeve of his T-shirt and pointed to the Marine insignia tattoo on his biceps. "Once a Marine, always a Marine."

"But you're not being deployed now," Jodie argued. "Any member of your team could settle down—if he wanted."

"We'll burn that bridge when we come to it," Jeff said. "Right now, we're focused on making Archer Farm work. We don't have wives, but tonight we'll have eleven boys in our care. Five more arrive in a week. That's all the family this team can handle for now."

Jodie scanned his features. Was he sending her a not-so-subtle message? Or had her raging hormones infused his simple statement with a signal he hadn't intended? Obviously his earlier kiss in the gazebo had been casual, at best, no strings attached. At any rate, she considered herself warned. Archer Farm left Jeff no time for her, except as a business partner.

And wasn't that what she wanted?

Before she could contemplate further, he said, "C'mon. I'll show you upstairs."

Across from the central front door, they climbed wide stairs to the second story where four huge bedrooms with four beds each had been painted in bright primary colors and furnished with coordinating spreads and curtains, cushioned chairs, study desks and foot lockers. On each end of the floor, a massive bathroom with walk-in showers sparkled with new porcelain fixtures.

"All the comforts of home," Jodie observed with approval.

"For most of these kids," Jeff said quietly, "this

dorm will be a step up from the homes they've known.''

Jodie couldn't help remembering Jeff's deprived childhood. No wonder he wanted these boys to have what he'd never known. "This is homey and practical, but without that institutional look.''

Jeff grinned. "That's what we were aiming for. Trace's sister is an interior decorator. We followed her advice.''

His megawatt smile made her stomach flip-flop. She drew in a deep breath and fought against the magnetic appeal of a man who cared deeply about children whom the rest of society wanted simply to lock away. Maybe fresh air would slow her galloping pulse. "Show me what you've done outside.''

She followed him out of the dorm and into the gardens, where they spoke briefly with Ricochet and Daniel and admired the first crop of lettuces almost ready for picking. Then they rounded the coop where the free-range chickens were settling in for the night and passed through the barn. The entire farm was immaculately clean, the crisp mountain air redolent with the scent of rich earth, fresh hay and flowers.

Beside the barn in the new, spanking-clean dairy with its tile floor and whitewashed walls, Kermit placed stainless-steel canisters of fresh milk into a huge refrigerator.

"This is quite an operation," Jodie said with admiration.

Kermit nodded. "We haven't started cheese production yet. But it won't be long now."

Jeff led Jodie out of the dairy and across the yard to a split-rail fence that enclosed the pasture. A goat kid left the herd and scampered over to greet them.

Jodie scratched the animal's head through the rails. "Does it have a name?"

"Gunny. After my gunnery sergeant at boot camp."

"Was the sergeant this cute?" The goat nuzzled her hand.

Jeff scowled. "He was a son of a...gun. And he smelled a whole lot worse than this little guy. Gunny, here, with his sweet disposition, is nothing like his namesake."

"Then why name him that?"

Jeff grinned. "For the satisfaction of knowing how ticked off Gunny would be if he knew."

The sun was sinking toward the rim of the western mountains, the air had chilled, and the sky had turned from blue to an amazing apricot. The sight filled Jodie with a quiet peace. Beside her, Jeff folded his arms on the top rail and gazed across the meadow, his expression thoughtful, and his profile, like the regal image on an old Roman coin, even more handsome than she'd remembered.

"You must be very proud of your farm," she said.

Jeff nodded. "I used to hate it. Couldn't wait to be anywhere but here. With the help of my team, though, we've changed it. It's a home now, a place I hope our clients will want to be.''

''It definitely beats prison.''

''That's the idea.'' He turned and looked at her. ''Will you answer a question?''

Guessing what he was about to say, she wished she had prepared an explanation. ''You're wondering why I changed my mind about accepting your business offer?''

His expression solemn, he shook his head. ''I want to know why you refused in the first place.''

Chapter Seven

Jeff's question caught Jodie by surprise, apparent in her swift intake of breath, the widening of her magnificent eyes and the sudden stillness of her hands. But he wasn't sorry he'd asked. He needed to know whether she still thought of him as the town pariah. If so, keeping their relationship strictly business would be a whole lot easier. Her prejudice would help banish her from his thoughts so he could concentrate on the challenges of Archer Farm without distraction.

She took forever to speak. A flurry of emotions scudded across her pretty features, and her face flushed as pink as a windblown rose. "I'm not sure I want to answer."

"Why not?"

"It's personal."

So, his suspicion that she still considered him an outcast was true, and even though he'd expected her attitude, he was disappointed. "I have a thick skin."

"But I don't." Sadness filled her eyes before she

looked away and focused on the flock of ducks, barely rippling the smooth surface of the pond with their sedate paddling.

Confusion gripped him. "I don't understand."

Continuing to avoid his gaze, she stared across the pasture. Her lower lip trembled with a sweet vulnerability. "Admitting that I'm not a good mother isn't easy."

"What?" Maybe she'd misunderstood his question. What did her status as a mother have to do with refusing his business deal?

"One reason I've wanted nothing to do with Archer Farms," she said softly, "is because of Brittany."

She looked so stricken, he wanted to pull her into his arms, hold her close and reassure her. Instead he kept his voice even to disguise how deeply her distress touched him. "What makes you think you're not a good mother?"

She leaned down, pulled a stem of meadow grass and wound it around her fingers. "When Brittany was much younger, she asked about her father. I told her he was dead."

"Is he?" Jeff couldn't help being curious. To his knowledge, no one in Pleasant Valley had ever identified the father of Jodie's child.

"I wouldn't lie to her, not about something that important," Jodie said. "But when Brittany entered her teens, she pressed me for more details."

Interested as he was, Jodie's extreme discomfort with the subject bothered him. "You don't have to tell me. Like you said, it's personal."

Jodie lifted her face and gave him a straightforward look. "I want to tell you. So you'll understand why I have to keep Brittany away from your farm and your clients. So you'll know it has nothing to do with you."

A weight in his heart lifted at her words, but he didn't want to add to her distress. "Tell me only if you're sure you want to."

"I'm sure." She took a deep breath, wiped her grass-stained fingers on her jeans, and continued. "When Brittany reached her teens, I told her everything. How I'd been a bashful, clumsy teen working in Daddy's store when Landry Mercer and his son Randy came in."

"*Senator* Landry Mercer?"

She nodded. "They were in Pleasant Valley for trout fishing and had rented a place on the river. Randy came into the store for supplies."

Jeff recalled that Mr. Nathan had always stocked a section of sporting goods in his hardware store, including fishing tackle and handmade flies.

"I was a high school freshman then," Jodie continued.

Jeff remembered. Jodie had been shy and not as mature as most girls her age, but she'd always had a sunny smile and a friendly hello, unlike others, who had shunned him entirely.

"Randy was a senior at his high school in Columbia," Jodie was saying. "Tall and athletic with blond hair and blue eyes, he was the best-looking boy I'd ever met. And most of all, he seemed interested in *me*. I was hooked faster than any fish he ever caught. And too young and naive to recognize that Randy didn't care about me. He was merely bored out of his skull with trout fishing and looking for other amusement."

Jeff frowned. He'd met plenty of Randy's type. Good-looking boys from wealthy, prominent families who felt entitled to whatever they wanted, no matter the cost or who they hurt in the process.

"To make a long story short," Jodie said, "I believed I was madly in love with Randy and thought he loved me. We saw a lot of each other, behind our parents' backs, of course, because I was under strict orders not to date until I was sixteen. One thing led to another, and...you can imagine my surprise and complete heartbreak when he returned to Columbia and I never heard from him again. But that surprise was nothing compared to the discovery that I was pregnant."

"That must have been tough," Jeff said, "especially in a small town like Pleasant Valley. I know firsthand how vicious gossip can be."

"Remaining here would have been impossible, if

not for my family. They stood by me with unconditional love. My parents contacted the senator, but he vigorously denied that Randy was the father of my child. He even accused them of attempting blackmail. Public acknowledgment of Randy's role would have been a political nightmare for the senator, so he made threats. To save me further embarrassment, my folks dropped the matter.''

"Never liked the man," Jeff said, liking the power-hungry senator even less now. "Never voted for him. Never will."

"The following year, after Brittany was born, Randy was killed in a car crash. He was a freshman at Clemson and driving drunk. I guess he felt invincible, knowing that no matter what mess he caused, his father would rescue him. But even the powerful Senator Mercer couldn't raise his son from the dead.''

"And you told all this to Brittany?"

Jodie nodded. "Once she was old enough and started asking probing questions, I answered them the best I could. I hoped that honesty was the best policy."

The devastation in her expression said otherwise. "And it wasn't?"

"It backfired. Big-time."

Touched by her anguish, Jeff slid his arm around her shoulders and pulled her against him. She was apparently too upset by her story to pull away, and he delighted in her softness. Her head barely reached his shoulder, and the setting sun brought out the high-lights in her hair. He pressed his cheek against her head and breathed in the subtle sweet fragrance of her magnolia shampoo, felt the rise and fall of her breathing against his chest and reveled in the perfection of the moment.

"How did it backfire?" he asked gently.

"A year ago Brittany decided to contact her grandfather. She was convinced that I'd somehow bungled things. That if I hadn't, her famous granddad would be happy to claim her."

Jodie leaned against him, and Jeff tightened his embrace. "I'm guessing things didn't turn out the way she wanted," he said.

She shook her head. "The senator refused to take her calls and never answered her letters."

"That must have been rough," Jeff murmured. He remembered how his father had ignored him, except when he had work for Jeff to do. Or was drunk and needed a punching bag. Being invisible hadn't been much of a self-esteem builder.

"Brit took the Senator's rejection hard. And again blamed it on me. She started acting out. You've probably noticed her Goth look."

Jeff shrugged. "If that's the worst of her problems…"

"It isn't. And, except for nixing tattoos and body piercing, I haven't objected to the way she dresses, hoping she'll eventually tire of it. But Brittany's gone far beyond violating dress codes. She started skipping school and hanging out with a rough group of kids at Carsons Corner. One stole a car a while back and took Brit and her friends for a joy ride. The highway patrol caught them.''

"Brittany has a record?" No wonder Jodie was edgy about his clients.

"No, but only because Chief Sawyer and Brynn intervened."

Jeff recalled Brynn's kindly father, the police chief who had tried without success to intercede on his behalf almost three decades ago. The chief who'd looked the other way when Jeff had made his moonshine deliveries, knowing the boy's father would beat him within an inch of his life if he didn't carry out his old man's wishes.

"Did her brush with the law teach her a lesson?" Jeff asked.

Jodie shook her head. "If anything, she's been worse. When Merrilee returned from New York last March, Brittany flattened her car tires and made anonymous threatening phone calls."

"Why?"

"She was angry at Merrilee for breaking Grant's heart years ago. And I have to believe Brit took satisfaction in intimidating my best friend."

"Sounds like your girl has a barn-size chip on her shoulder." Jeff felt for Jodie, but he could also understand where Brittany was coming from, a place Jeff knew well from his own growing up.

"She's been on restriction ever since the stolen car incident," Jodie said, "which hasn't exactly improved our relationship. Brittany still blames me for all her problems, her alienation from her paternal grandparents, her separation from her friends." She forced a weak smile. "Sometimes she even blames me for the weather and the lack of good shows on TV."

"Have you considered counseling?" Jeff asked.

"That's my next step."

"Maybe you could talk to Gofer," he suggested.

She shook her head. "I won't impose. He's going to have his hands full."

Jeff placed his hands on her shoulders and rotated her to face him. "Thank you for sharing your concerns about Brittany. I'll do everything in my power to keep my program from impacting her negatively."

Jodie stared up at him with a sad, little smile. "Thanks for understanding."

"That's what friends are for."

Her smile widened then. "Are we?"

"What?"

"Friends?"

"You've been my friend for longer than you know." He cursed the huskiness in his voice and garnered his self-restraint to keep from kissing her again. "Ever since high school."

"I barely knew you then."

He brushed the back of his hand against the curve of her cheek, soft as a sun-ripe peach. "You were the only girl in school who ever spoke to me. I know it sounds crazy, but your friendly hellos meant a lot."

FRIENDS.

Remembering Sunday's conversation with her mother, Jodie groaned and pulled away from Jeff.

"What's wrong?" he asked.

"You're going to need all the friends you can get."

"I have friends," he said with a dazzling grin and a gesture that took in the entire farm. "The best friends a man could want."

She shook her head. "You need more than your team. You need friends in town. Powerful friends."

"Why?"

Her heart sank. If he didn't know about the petition, she'd be the bearer of very bad news. And she hoped he wouldn't shoot the messenger.

A wave of dizziness washed over her. She'd read somewhere that infatuation changes brain chemistry. Her obsession had definitely fried the circuits in her brain. She'd already blabbed her life story, and here she was spilling the latest town gossip. Usually referred to by her family as the quiet one, she had suddenly transformed into a regular Chatty Cathy.

Since she'd brought up the allusion to the petition,

however, she couldn't back out now. "You haven't heard about the petition?"

His smile faded and his gray eyes turned dark as a night sky. "What petition?"

"The one circulating at Grant's reception. I didn't know about it either, until Mama mentioned it yesterday."

Jeff leaned backward against the fence and propped his elbows on the top rail. But his casual posture didn't fool her. His phenomenal self-control couldn't hide the slight tick in his right cheek, the pulse throbbing in the vein at his neck or the heat lightning in his eyes. He had the stillness of a predator, poised to attack.

"What does the petition say?" His tone was hard, cold, like lava that had solidified to cover boiling magma beneath its crust.

"I haven't seen it," she admitted, "but I heard it's a request for a county ordinance to ban Archer Farm's operation as a rehabilitation facility."

Get to know him, her mother had said. *Get him out of your system.* How long, Jodie wondered, before familiarity bred distance? The more she was around him, the more she liked him. Compassion flooded her for the man whose dream was threatened, and, more than anything, she wanted to reach out and touch him.

"I have the proper permits." Jeff's words were clipped and crisp, as if he held back what he really wanted to say. "Our attorney assured me we've met all the legal requirements."

The muscle in his cheek ticked faster. Military men were infamous for their wide vocabulary of curses, and Jodie guessed that Jeff had to be exercising tremendous control to keep from swearing. She'd be cussing up a blue streak if someone had launched a petition to shut down her café.

"Maybe the petition will die from lack of signatures," she said.

"And maybe the sun will rise in the west tomorrow," he said with a sigh of resignation. "You know how people in this county feel about us Davidsons."

"You're not your father," Jodie reminded him.

He shoved away from the fence. "And I can't worry about things I have no control over. My best weapon against this petition is to prove the project can be successful. We'd better get to work."

"Work?" She blinked in surprise.

"We have an agreement to draw up," he said. "That's why you're here."

"Of course," she mumbled, and followed him to the farmhouse with cheeks flaming, all too aware that his sympathetic listening and unsettling proximity had addled her mind until she'd forgotten why she came.

EARLY THE NEXT MORNING, Jeff parked on Piedmont Avenue and scanned the town that, with the exception of Jodie's place, hadn't changed in the years he'd been away. With its early-twentieth-century brick storefronts, wide tree-lined sidewalks, and sleepy two-lane main drag, the street seemed caught in a time warp.

Before leaving Pleasant Valley to join the Marines, Jeff had hated the town with a white-hot passion, had found the attitudes of its inhabitants suffocating, its locale provincial, its lack of possibilities depressing, its unspoken hostilities unbearable.

Once he'd left, however, he'd undergone an unexpected transformation. Lying in his barracks bunk late at night at the Parris Island boot camp, he'd been stricken with a fierce homesickness, not for his father or the farm, but for the familiar town and Mr. and Mrs. Weatherstone. Later, hiding in the underbrush on a freezing, windswept slope of an Afghan mountain, facedown in the sands of an Iraqi desert, or deployed in any of a dozen countries where he'd risked his life, he'd longed for the peace, tranquility, and predictability of Pleasant Valley. In the long, tension-filled waiting to complete dangerous missions, memories of the Weatherstones' many kindnesses, the gentle encouragement of Cat Stratton, his English teacher, and the willingly blind eye of crusty old Chief Sawyer to Jeff's teenage transgressions had often thawed his heart from the icy fear that gripped it.

While in the service, Jeff had believed that his homesickness sprang merely from the fact that he couldn't return, not as long as his father lived. But now, standing on the main street, his longing fulfilled, he couldn't deny his contentment at coming home or the overwhelming sensation that he was exactly where he belonged.

He studied the scene that he'd envisioned so often in his daydreams. On the north side of the main street stood Paulie's Drugstore, Amy Lou Baker's beauty shop with its catchy name, The Hair Apparent, and Fulton's Department Store. Jay-Jay's Garage and the First Baptist Church flanked the row of stores like bookends.

On the street's south side, shaded by tall maples that flamed red and gold in the fall, were Brynn's uncle Bud's real estate office, First National Bank, Nathan's Hardware, Mountain Crafts and Café, Blalock's Grocery and the Pleasant Valley Community Church, where Grant had married Merrilee last Saturday night. Behind these buildings the Piedmont River ran, close to overflowing its steep banks with the runoff from early-summer rains.

On the town's east end, the street curved uphill out of sight, but in his mind's eyes, Jeff pictured city hall, the hospital and medical clinic, the public school complex on the left, and the police and fire stations on the right, just past the lumberyard. Located well off the main highways, Pleasant Valley had been spared so far from an invasion of fast-food franchises, monstrous shopping malls, and gigantic one-stop home-improvement stores.

Waiting for Daniel to return from the department store, Jeff twisted on the front seat of his pickup for a better view of the café. The building was a far cry from the dilapidated, dusty fix-it shop where, as a young boy, he'd spent many happy hours with Mr. Weatherstone as his instructor. The old man had taught him woodworking, electrical wiring and, Jeff's favorite, rebuilding and tuning engines. He'd also taught Jeff to curb the nasty outbursts of temper he had learned so well from his father. Today, except for original outlines of the old shop, nothing about it looked the same.

Jodie had added log siding to the front for a rustic touch, and a jaunty awning of burgundy and dark-green striped canvas protected the double door entry. The glass panes of the door and the huge display windows on either side, formerly opaque with grime, sparkled in the early-morning sun. Dew clung to the cheery red petunias, frothy white alyssum and plumes of fountain grasses grouped in massive redwood pots that flanked the doorway.

The same arrangements were repeated in redwood flower boxes at the second-floor windows of the apartment where Jodie and Brittany lived, rooms Mr. Weatherstone had used only for storage.

Brittany, Jeff thought, was a wild child, just as he had been, and for not-so-different reasons. Although she had the full love and support of the Nathans, Jodie had revealed yesterday that Brittany was not only unwanted by her father's family, the Mercers refused even to acknowledge their kinship. Jeff had intended to consult Gofer last night about the girl's dilemma and consequent rebelliousness, but once the bus had arrived with ten frightened, surly and generally un-disciplined teenagers, the entire team had had their hands full.

Jeff had been walking Jodie to her van just as the bus had pulled in and disgorged its load. Her eyes had widened in unmistakable horror when the boys climbed off in their hip-hop clothes, some skinheads, others with dreadlocks or do-rags, and all sprouting so much metal from body piercings that they resem-bled walking pin cushions. Correction: *tattooed* pin cushions. Any one of them would have been the worst nightmare of the mother of a teenage daughter.

After that, Jodie hadn't been able to leave fast enough, he recalled with a frown. He'd been glad she'd already agreed to hire Daniel. If not, she might have lost her nerve at the sight of the "terrible ten" and backed out of her freshly inked agreement with Archer Farm.

To make certain she hadn't changed her mind over-night, Jeff had wakened Daniel at oh-dark-hundred, hustled him into town, and had him standing tall out-side Fulton's Department Store hours before their nine-o'clock opening time. Fortunately, Tom Fulton kept his father's old habit of working in the store before it opened. He'd answered Jeff's knock and, after hearing what Daniel required, let the boy in to make his purchases.

A rap on the truck window startled Jeff from his thoughts. Daniel stood by the driver's door, looking awkward but neat in the black slacks and white polo shirt Jodie required as uniform for her busboys. A plastic Fulton's bag dangling from his hand held the clothes he'd worn to town.

Jeff hopped out. "Toss that bag in the truck and let me have a look at you."

Daniel did as he was told, then squirmed under Jeff's scrutiny. "Am I okay?"

Jeff's heart twisted at the boy's uncertainty and his obvious desire to please. "You're more than okay, Daniel. You look great. Ms. Nathan is lucky to have a guy like you working for her. I know you'll do your best. Ready?"

After a self-conscious smoothing of his bright-red cowlick that promptly sprang upright after the swipe of his hand, Daniel nodded.

"Let's go." Jeff draped his arm around the kid's shoulders and walked him toward the café entrance. "Just do what Ms. Nathan says, remember to say please and thank you, and you'll be fine."

"Yes, sir. Thank you, sir."

Jeff opened the door and stepped inside. A melange of smells—freshly ground coffee, sausage grilling and the cinnamon aroma of baked goods—enveloped him and made his stomach rumble. He'd eaten hours ago.

He scanned the front room for Jodie. The tables and counter stools were filled with the Tuesday-morning breakfast crowd, but she was nowhere in sight.

Jeff caught the attention of Maria, the dark-haired, dark-eyed, young short-order cook behind the counter, who was flipping an omelet.

"Where's Jodie?" he called over the hubbub of a dozen conversations.

Maria jerked her thumb toward the back of the building, looked past Jeff and eyed Daniel with obvious skepticism.

"Follow me," Jeff said to Daniel, who'd broken into a sweat at the sight of so many strangers.

He led the boy through the gift shop area to the deck at the back of the building, another of Jodie's innovations. Huge glass panels arched over the structure, shielding patrons from the elements while offering a panoramic view of the river, rushing past a hundred feet away, and the mountains in the distance. Today the panels were open to admit the fresh summer breeze.

The deck tables were empty except for one at the far corner, where Jodie sat with Brittany, who was apparently finishing breakfast. When Jodie glimpsed Jeff and Daniel, surprise flashed across her features before she settled them into a welcoming smile and waved the new arrivals over.

"You two are out early," she said.

"Daniel's reporting for work, dress code and all.

Looks good, doesn't he?'' He pleaded with his eyes for Jodie not to reject the boy.

He needn't have worried. The smile she gave Daniel projected maternal approval. ''I don't know, Daniel. Can't have my busboys so good-looking they distract the customers.''

Daniel blushed, and Jeff couldn't help wondering how little positive reinforcement the kid had received in his life.

''Hi, Brittany,'' Jeff said. ''I haven't had a chance to thank you for your help at our place last month. It was dirty, grungy work, and I appreciate your giving us a hand.''

''No sweat.'' Brittany looked both pleased and embarrassed by his gratitude. She turned to her mother. ''May I show Daniel what he's supposed to do?''

Jeff had to admire Jodie's self-restraint. In spite of her concern about Daniel's influence on her impressionable daughter, she didn't flinch but answered with genuine warmth. ''Of course. You'll make a good teacher. Brit's been waiting tables some since school ended,'' Jodie explained to Jeff. ''She knows almost as much about the business as I do.''

''C'mon, Daniel,'' Brittany, also dressed in black slacks and a white polo shirt, pushed to her feet. ''We'll find you an apron.''

The teens went inside, and Jodie gestured to the place across from hers. ''I'm finishing my coffee. Want a cup?''

Jeff sat, and Jodie took a clean cup and saucer from a serving counter nearby. She poured steaming liquid from a carafe on the table and offered him a muffin from a linen-draped basket. With his appetite already stimulated by the café's delicious odors, he couldn't refuse. He broke it in two, took a bite and was glad he hadn't declined. Sweetness, texture and flavor exploded in his mouth.

"Man, these are incredible. You make them?"

Jodie nodded. "Pecan and cranberry. My own special recipe."

He noted the stack of folders on the table in front of her and read a few of their labels upside down: receipts, payables, inventory, payroll, taxes. From his short stint as Archer Farm's administrator, he'd learned paperwork could be a full-time job.

"When do you find time to bake?" He took another bite and noticed the half-moon smudges of fatigue beneath her long lower lashes.

"In the afternoons and evenings, when the café's closed."

"In between paperwork?" He nodded toward the folders at her elbow.

She shrugged. "Running a business is a full-time job. Especially a café that's open seven days a week."

"Raising a teenager is a full-time job, too. As my team and I are only beginning to discover." He felt a hitch in his heart for Jodie, who'd missed the opportunity to be a teenager. She'd been raising Brittany instead. "What do you do for fun?"

She laughed. "I don't have energy left for fun. I'm grateful if I have a few hours a week to put my feet up and zone out with the television."

"You work too hard. You should take more time off."

"You sound like my mother."

"Your mother's right."

"But my mother doesn't have all this to worry about, or Brittany, either." She fixed him with a stare. "I'm taking a chance with your Daniel, you know."

"I promise you won't be sorry."

"And I'll hold you to that promise," she said forcefully. She set down her cup and began stacking her folders. "Now, I have work to do."

"Whoa, not so fast."

"You may have all day to dawdle, but I don't."

"I made you a promise. Now I want you to make me one."

"Yesterday wasn't enough?" Her brow wrinkled in obvious puzzlement. "Seems like I signed a gazillion papers."

"That was business." He worked to keep his tone light so she wouldn't see how strongly she'd affected him, wouldn't guess at the wave of protectiveness that had engulfed him out of the blue. With the clarity of a lightning bolt, he realized that he wanted to take care of Jodie Nathan, to ease her worries, make her laugh, lighten her workload and brighten the endless drudgery of her days.

And he wanted to kiss her again. And again. Until all those kisses led to more. Much more. He'd never experienced such a mixture of tenderness and desire toward any other woman and had to clear his throat before he could speak.

"That was business," he repeated. "This is pleasure."

She gazed at him suspiciously and asked with a strange little wobble in her voice, "What's pleasure?"

He focused on the dimple in her left cheek to keep his mind from careering off into a dozen equally seductive fantasies. Jodie was nothing if not terminally practical. If she had any idea the direction his thoughts were taking, he'd scare her away for good.

"I'm offering you a day off. With no responsibilities."

"Ha! That's not pleasure, it's an impossibility." She stood, picked up her file folders and held them against her chest like a shield. He felt an irrational stab of envy for the folders.

"It's not going to happen," she added emphatically.

"Why not?"

"Look," she said with a reasonable tone that might have discouraged a less motivated man, "you have four guys to take up the slack when you're not at

Archer Farm. Otherwise, you wouldn't be here now, right?''

He nodded, unable to refute her.

"There's only one of me," she continued.

One of Jodie was all he needed. More than he'd ever wanted.

"And what happens if you burn out?" he asked. "Or let yourself get so run-down that you catch something and are too sick to work? You owe it to yourself to take time off. It's good business sense."

"Point taken. When I've figured out how to clone myself, I'll take a vacation." She turned to leave.

"Wait." He was keeping her from her work but enjoying her company too much to let her go. "If I can figure out a way to free some of your time, will you promise to spend a day with me?"

"Sure," she said with a saucy grin that infused him with hope until she added, "and buy me a lottery ticket while you're at it."

He ignored her sarcasm and glommed on to her initial agreement. "You promise? One full day?"

This time she laughed out loud. "My first free day is at least four years away, after Brittany leaves for college. If you don't mind waiting that long—"

"I'm betting within the next two weeks," he said. And he wasn't laughing.

She shook her head in disbelief. "Not unless you're a miracle worker."

"Ah, how quickly you forget," he chided her.

"Forget what?"

"I'm a Marine. We're trained to do the impossible. I'll fulfill my end of the bargain. Be prepared to keep yours."

Jeff strode past her and noted with satisfaction her soft lips, parted in surprise; the swirling fragrance of magnolias; her appealing blush; and the fact that he'd struck her speechless.

When he entered the main dining room, Daniel and Brittany were clearing tables for the waiting crowd. Daniel worked with such quiet efficiency, his forehead knotted in concentration, that he didn't notice Jeff's approach.

"You doing okay?" Jeff asked.

"Yes, sir," the boy answered. "It's even kinda fun, working with Brittany and all."

"Someone will pick you up this afternoon."

"I could hitch a ride."

Jeff shook his head. "Against the rules, remember?"

"Yes, sir." Daniel's expression was earnest, and Jeff recalled Gofer describing the boy as an eager puppy dog. "I didn't intend to break a rule, sir. I only wanted to spare you the trouble."

Jeff placed his hand on the boy's shoulder and gave a reassuring squeeze. "You're no trouble, son. The staff at Archer Farm is here for you. Always."

"I won't let you down."

"I know, or you wouldn't have this job. I trust you, Daniel. Remember that."

With a farewell wave to Brittany, Jeff went out the door.

Climbing into his truck, he wondered why he felt so confident. He'd pledged Jodie the impossible, and he hadn't a clue how he'd deliver on that promise.

But as he'd said, he was a Marine. He'd think of something.

Chapter Eight

Brittany slid the last plate into the apartment's dishwasher and closed the door. "Can I go now?"

"Go?" Jodie asked. "You're still on restriction."

"Sheesh, Mom, only to my room. I want to paint my nails."

Jodie smothered a grimace at the sight of her daughter's black-tipped fingers. "You did them last night."

"But I bought new polish today."

"More black?"

"Pink." At Brittany's blush, Jodie realized that her daughter's face lacked its usual unnatural pallor from dead-white makeup. "Daniel said he liked the way I looked at Uncle Grant's wedding."

Jodie held her tongue and thanked God for small favors. She'd worried that Daniel with his juvenile record would be a bad influence, but if he'd encouraged Brittany to abandon her walking-dead look, Jodie would be forever in the boy's debt. "You were beautiful at the wedding, cupcake, the prettiest girl there.''

''Oh, yeah? What about Merrilee?''

''She had an unfair advantage. Bridal gown, billowing veil, radiant smile, and happiness oozing from every pore. But you were still spectacular.'' Jodie's eyes threatened to tear at the memory of her daughter, so lovely in her bridesmaid's dress and so fast approaching the threshold of adulthood. ''I was so proud of you. And not only for your looks. Pretty is—''

''—as pretty does.'' With a smile, Brittany finished another of Sophie Nathan's favorite sayings. Grandma's homespun wisdom formed a common bond between them.

Brit's smile faded, and her customary pout returned. ''So am I excused?''

Jodie longed for a real dialogue with her daughter. When they talked, she often felt more like a prosecuting attorney interrogating a witness than a mom. Not that she expected to be Brittany's friend. With her own mother as an example, she knew that her job, first and foremost, was to parent. And a good parent kept the lines of communication open. But a heart-to-heart chat with her daughter obviously wasn't going to happen tonight.

''Go ahead,'' Jodie said. ''I'm almost through here.''

Brittany made her escape, and Jodie finished cleaning the kitchen island that overlooked the family room at the back of the apartment. When she'd renovated the spacious upstairs into living quarters, Mrs. Weatherstone's low asking price had left Jodie with enough equity to splurge on floor-to-ceiling windows that overlooked a small balcony and the river and mountains beyond. The glass expanse and high ceilings added openness and airiness to an otherwise claustrophobic space.

That afternoon, she and Brittany had worked late downstairs, dusting the gift shop shelves and mopping and polishing the floors. Luckily, Maria had left them supper, Caesar salads with grilled chicken, in the café refrigerator, because they'd been too tired to cook. Brittany's labor, at least, was over for the day. Jodie still had to tally receipts and prepare tomorrow's bank statement.

She welcomed the practical distraction from her whirling thoughts. Clearing Jeff from her system by getting to know him wasn't working. Familiarity hadn't bred the hoped-for contempt. Instead, every time Jodie was near him, like yesterday morning when he'd brought Daniel for his first day at work, Jeff's presence merely increased her desire to have him around more often. As much as the admission frightened her, she had to accept that her infatuation was developing into something deeper, more substantive.

And that scared her even more than the physical

desire he'd stirred in her. She'd had one disastrous sexual encounter in her life. But she'd had absolutely zero experience in falling in love. Her growing feelings for Jeff made her so crazy that one minute she never wanted to see him again and the next, she longed for his company so much she ached.

After his crazy promise to ease her workload so she could spend a day with him, she'd expected him at least to seek her out and speak to her this morning when he'd dropped off Daniel—along with crates of freshly picked lettuces, herbs and eggs from the farm. But Jeff had come and gone before Jodie had realized he'd been there.

And when she'd learned that he'd left without even saying hello, she hadn't known whether to feel relieved or annoyed. Definitely relieved, she decided now. If Jeff brought Daniel and supplies every morning, she'd be better off not encountering the tantalizing ex-Marine on a regular basis. If her infatuation really was developing into deeper feelings, maybe avoiding him could head them off.

The telephone rang, most likely one of Brittany's friends calling. She let her daughter answer the phone in her bedroom. If Jodie didn't tackle her paperwork now, she'd be up all night.

"Mom," Brit hollered from her room that fronted the main street, "it's for you."

Wishing she'd insisted that the answering machine take the call, Jodie grabbed the kitchen extension. She didn't have time to chat, and the only people who ever phoned, besides Merrilee, who was on her honeymoon, were her mother and Brynn, both marathon talkers.

"Just calling to see if you're home." Jeff's deep voice filled her ear.

"Obviously," Jodie dryly, "or I wouldn't be answering this line."

"Then you'd better open your front door."

"What?"

"I'm downstairs on my cell phone. I have a delivery."

"The café's closed for the night."

"It's not for the café. It's for you."

"I haven't ordered anything."

"Remember my promise?"

She grinned. He'd promised the impossible, to ease her workload, and had come to admit defeat. "Backing out?"

"Marines never retreat. I'm here to keep that promise. Will you let me in?"

Jodie had the perfect excuse. "I can't. I still have the day's receipts to add up—"

"All the more reason you need what I've brought. Besides, the ice cream's melting."

"Ice cream?"

"Homemade with fresh cream and wild blueberries."

Jeff's voice was seductive, enticing, and a physical hunger curled in Jodie's stomach.

"Trace made it," he said, "and the ice it's packed in won't last forever."

"I really do have to work."

"Eat some ice cream, see what I've brought and then you can throw me out, if you like. I won't take much of your time."

Unable to think of further excuses, Jodie hung up the receiver and sprinted downstairs toward the café's entrance. Through the double doors she had a full view of Jeff, standing in the summer twilight. He looked more handsome than any man had a right to with his bronzed face lit by the setting sun, his hair tousled by the wind, his broad shoulders straining the fabric of his windbreaker, snug jeans molding his thighs, and each hand holding a bulging shopping bag.

Dizziness assaulted her. If Jeff was eye candy, she'd just suffered a sugar overdose.

She unlocked the door and nodded toward the bags. "Looks like you brought enough ice cream for a Marine platoon."

His face broke into a smile that warmed the cool gray of his eyes, produced a fine web of wrinkles at their corners and sent a shiver of delight down her spine. "You can never have too much ice cream."

"Spoken like a true man. Women worry about the calories going straight to their hips." She stood aside for him to enter, locked the door behind him and preceded him up the stairs to the apartment. She could feel his laser gaze locked on her back.

"From my point of view—" approval heated his voice "—the ice cream's no threat. Your hips look just fine."

Jodie suppressed a groan. She still wore the grubby jeans and faded shirt in which she'd cleaned the floors, and her hair looked as if she'd styled it in a hurricane. Just as well that she wasn't dressed to kill, she assured herself. If she didn't want to encourage Jeff, he might as well view her at her worst. Maybe then he'd give up his ridiculous crusade to spend time with her.

At the top of the stairs she stepped to one side and motioned him into the family room. "You can put the bags on the kitchen island."

He set down the plastic carryalls and glanced around. His eyes widened with apparent surprise. "This is a great space. Your view's incredible. Last time I was in this room, it was filled with junk, old furniture, appliance parts and newspapers. Mr. Weatherstone never threw anything away."

"Unfortunately, that unpleasant task was left to me." Jodie glanced at the bag. "Should I put the ice cream in the freezer?"

"What ice cream?" Brittany, waving her hands to dry her nail polish, came up the hall. "Hi, Mr. Davidson."

"Hi, Brittany." Jeff reached into the first bag and removed a gallon-size Tupperware container. "Trace made ice cream. Remember that pool in the creek behind our place?"

"The one with the tadpoles?"

Jeff nodded. "We found wild blueberries growing along the banks. Trace added them to the ice cream. Want a sample?"

"Sure." Brittany hesitated and looked to Jodie. "Is it okay, Mom?"

Jodie had hoped to refrigerate the dessert and send Jeff on his way, but Brittany had worked so hard today, Jodie couldn't deny her daughter the treat. "Get bowls, a scoop and some spoons. Mr. Davidson can serve."

"First things first." Jeff dug into the second bag and retrieved two bouquets of flowers. He handed Jodie a profusion of red and gold zinnias, yellow snapdragons and old-fashioned coral roses. "For you."

"They're lovely." Jodie buried her nose in the fragrant blossoms to hide her surprise at his gift.

"They're from Ricochet," Jeff added. "He wanted me to ask if you'd like him to provide flowers for the café tables."

Jodie mentally smacked herself for misinterpreting the bouquet. The flowers weren't a symbol of Jeff's feelings, just another business proposition. "I'll consider it," she said.

Jeff presented the second bouquet, an arrangement

of pink phlox, Queen Anne's lace and pale-pink roses to Brittany. "Daniel sent you these."

Brittany's face matched the rosy hue of the flowers. "He did?"

"They're a thank-you," Jeff explained, "for teaching him the ropes in the café." He reached deeper into the second bag for two slim plastic boxes. "And I brought you these for making Daniel feel welcome. I appreciate your kindness toward him. He hasn't known much kindness in his life."

Brittany eyed the compact disks skeptically. "You picked those out?"

Jeff laughed and shook his head. "They're not elevator music, if that's what you're thinking. Daniel told me what to buy."

Brittany accepted the CDs and studied the covers. "Wow, they're exactly what I would have picked. Thanks."

"Now—" Jeff removed his windbreaker and tossed it on a chair "—time for ice cream."

Brittany quickly thrust her flowers into a water-filled vase, placed it on the island, and rummaged through the cabinets and drawers to find bowls and spoons.

Events were progressing too fast for Jodie. She couldn't remember the last time, if ever, a man had brought her flowers. After she'd thought about it, she realized Jeff could have simply asked about the table flowers, but he'd brought her a bouquet, too.

And never had one of her infrequent male friends included a gift for Brittany. Jodie laid her flowers on the counter and sank onto the nearest stool. Her thoughts whirled like a sky diver in free fall as she tried to comprehend Jeff's motives. Maybe, with her brain fried by overactive hormones and too tired to think clearly, she was making something out of nothing.

Jeff removed a smaller container from the ice-filled Tupperware, mounded ice cream from it into a bowl and handed the first serving to Brittany.

"May I take mine to my room and listen to my new CDs?" Brittany asked.

Jodie nodded. "But please keep the volume down—or use your head phones."

Brittany returned to her room. Jeff handed Jodie a bowl of ice cream with an ardent look that placed the concoction at risk of turning instantly to mush. She took a taste and almost moaned with delight at the rich cream melting on her tongue. "This is so good it has to be sinful."

Jeff grinned. "If the way to a man's heart is through his stomach, what with equal rights for women, I thought this worth a try."

Was he trying to win her heart? God, he was even more dangerous than she'd feared. She tried to make light of his admission. "Ply women with sweets, and they may hate you in the morning," she warned.

"Why?" he asked.

"Because of the jump in the reading on the bathroom scales." Jodie took another bite and savored the sweetness of the blueberries.

The warmth in Jeff's eyes kicked up a notch. "As hard as you work, and with your own private Stairmaster—" he nodded toward the steps that led to the café "—you'll never have to worry about your weight."

Jodie consumed another spoonful and swore to herself not to mention weight again. Jeff would think she obsessed over it, when she was merely latching onto the handiest safe topic of conversation.

He served himself, placed the remaining dessert in her freezer as casually as if he'd been a frequent visitor to her kitchen, and perched on the stool across the island from her.

"So," he said after a mouthful of the ice cream, "how's Daniel doing?"

Jodie couldn't help smiling. "He's the best busboy I've ever had. Conscientious, dependable, polite. I can't figure whether that's his true nature or he's just trying to impress Brit."

"That's one hundred percent Daniel. Gofer compares him to a puppy dog, eager to please. Seems all the kid really needed was people who believe in him."

"And your other clients?" Jodie tried not to shudder at the memory of the fierce, rebellious teens who'd joined Daniel last Sunday at Archer Farm. "Are they shaping up as well as Daniel?"

Jeff gazed past her toward the windows. "Too soon to tell."

What he hadn't said spoke volumes, and Jodie assumed Jeff and his team had their work cut out for them. "Shouldn't you be helping out at the farm?"

"It's movie night. That's why Trace made ice cream. Along with a DVD and popcorn, it's the boys' treat for a good day's work. The team can handle them."

She dropped her spoon in her bowl and set the dish aside. "You were nice to share this, but I really have to work."

"No problem." He pushed away his bowl and reached into the bottom of the second bag. "That's why I'm here. To help with your work."

"It's pretty much a one-person job." She stood and moved toward the door, hoping he would take the hint and leave.

He remained ensconced on the stool and waved the CD he'd retrieved from the bag. "That's where this comes in."

She shook her head. "I don't listen to music while I work. It interferes with my concentration."

"This isn't music." His gaze caressed her with unspoken promises. "Although that's not a bad idea for next time."

He looked so appealing, sitting in the middle of her

kitchen with his boyish grin and disheveled hair, she wanted to go to him, wrap her arms around his waist and bury her head on his shoulder.

A head that needed serious examining, apparently.

Those feelings had caused her big trouble in the past, and she struggled to apply the brakes to them. When other teens had been learning the nuances of male/female relationships, indulging in flirtations, adolescent crushes, prom nights and other dates, Jodie had been changing diapers and reading *Pat the Bunny* to Brittany before tackling her homework. With the responsibilities of her child, school and then her business, Jodie had never found much opportunity to fill in the gaps in her dating experience. She was perfectly comfortable with her father and brother, but after her experience with the Mercers, she remained wary of men and clueless over how to relate to them.

Aware of her ineptitude and her terrifying fear of commitment, her warm response to Jeff was all the more reason to get rid of him. Fast.

"There won't be a next time," she corrected. "I told you, I'm a workaholic."

"This is your antidote." He tossed her the CD.

She fumbled before catching it, then flipped the plastic sleeve over and read the title. "A computer program?"

"The best available for small businesses. I use it at the farm to keep up with inventory, payroll, everything."

"Maybe I don't have a computer," she hedged.

"But you do," he said with a knowing nod, "although all you use it for is e-mail and Web access."

His accuracy shocked her. "You sure you weren't with military intelligence? How do you know all this?"

"Daniel's my spy, and he's successfully infiltrated your organization." He spread his hands wide, and his grin turned sheepish. "In other words, he pumped Brittany for information."

Jodie hoped Brittany hadn't also blabbed how technically challenged her mother was, or the pathetic number of hours Jodie spent playing computer solitaire.

"Thanks for the offer." She tried to give the disk back. "I don't do computers."

He refused to accept the CD. "But I do. And the program's very simple. I'll load it and show you how to use it. Once you've got the hang of it, it will save you hours a week."

She arched an eyebrow. "Hours I can spend with you?"

"You only owe me a day." He shrugged. "So far."

"Are all Marines this cocky?"

"It's a requirement, ma'am. Recruiters check for it, first thing."

"You must have passed with flying colors."

"Head of the class. So let me load the program for you."

Jodie hesitated. Her home office was in the corner of her bedroom, the last place she wanted to take Jeff in her present state of out-of-her-mind. "Just leave it with me and I'll figure it out."

He stood, folded his arms across his muscular chest, leaned back against the kitchen counter with one booted foot resting on the lower cabinet door, and shook his head. "Your figuring it out defeats the entire purpose."

Her mouth went dry, and the heat in his eyes prevented her from asking exactly what his purpose was.

"If you have to load it," he said with irritating rationality, "and go through all those time-consuming, boring tutorials, you won't be freeing up time for that day with me."

"There's no hurry," she said quickly.

"But there is. I've already picked the day. A week from Saturday."

"No way. Saturday's one of our busiest days."

"I'm sure there's someone who covers for you occasionally." His smile was innocent but his eyes were wicked. "Like your mother?"

Jodie sighed. She did occasionally manage a day off, if and when she wanted it. Her allegedly full schedule was a ploy to keep Jeff at arm's length, a goal even more urgent as she recognized that she was becoming emotionally attached as well as physically attracted to the man. Unfortunately, her don't-have-time strategy wasn't working. "Is there anything Brittany *hasn't* told Daniel?"

His smoldering look threatened to send her into meltdown. "There're a few things I'd like to discover for myself."

On dangerous ground, she quickly changed the subject. "Why a week from Saturday?"

"The local bike club is having a poker run."

"I don't know how to play poker."

"You don't have to. The riders follow a designated route. At stops along the way, each participant draws a card. At the final stop, the rider with the best poker hand wins. No skill needed."

She blinked in surprise. "You want me to ride a motorcycle?"

He grinned. "I'll do the driving. All you have to do is hang on. It's for a good cause. The entry fees raise money for Christmas gifts for needy kids. We do another run during the holidays to deliver them."

Spend a day with her arms wrapped around Jeff? She liked the idea so much, it had to be a bad one. "I'm not the motorcycle type."

He laughed. "You don't have to be a biker babe to participate. Brynn's going. So are her uncle Bud and aunt Marion."

Bud Sawyer, local real estate agent and head of the Chamber of Commerce, and his wife Marion had ridden their BMW cycle as long as Jodie could remember. They swore the only way to appreciate the beauty of the Blue Ridge Parkway and other mountain routes was by motorcycle. But Brynn? "Did Brynn buy a bike?"

Jeff shook his head. "She's riding with another officer. Some guy with the Walhalla department whose name I can't remember."

"This entire discussion is moot," Jodie reminded him. "As I said before, I don't have time for a day off."

He moved closer, so near his scent of spicy soap and fresh mountain air teased her nostrils. Waggling the CD in front of her, he dared, "Afraid to give this a try?"

Rising to his challenge, she answered without thinking. "The computer's in the bedroom."

She spun on her heel and marched down the hall, praying she hadn't left underwear strewn across the bedroom furniture.

Jeff followed and almost bumped into her when she stopped abruptly on the threshold. Her queen-size bed with its handmade candlewick spread and profusion of pillows loomed large in the center of the room beneath the double windows, conjuring up images of twisted sheets and naked limbs. Thrusting the sensual thoughts aside, with brisk efficiency, she stepped into the room, skirted the bed and hurried to the corner desk where her computer sat.

She gestured to the chair in front of it.

With a fluid motion, as if straddling a bike, Jeff flung his leg across the chair, sat and inserted the CD in the disk drive. His long, capable fingers flew across the keyboard, and commands and information scrolled across the monitor.

But Jodie wasn't watching the screen. She couldn't tear her gaze from the back of his neck and the tantalizing strip of tanned skin visible between his collar and hairline. To break the spell, she stumbled backward and sat on the bed. God help her, she was losing her mind. She had to get this man out of her bedroom before she did something she'd regret in the morning. Only the presence of Brittany next door kept Jodie from flinging herself at Jeff.

She inhaled a deep, calming breath. "Finished?"

"Almost." The clatter of keys and Jeff's steady breathing filled the silence. "Got it."

He stood, reached for her hand and tugged her into the chair he'd vacated. "Your turn."

Bending over her with his arms around her to guide her hands over the keys, his cheek next to hers as he studied the screen, and his warm breath, fragrant with vanilla from the ice cream, mingling with hers, he took her through the steps of the business records program.

He might as well have been speaking Swahili.

"See," he said when he'd finished. "Easy as falling off a log."

"Right," she lied. She'd fallen all right. Fallen

hard. She stood quickly, only to find her nose against his broad chest. Caught in a tender trap between him and the desk chair, she couldn't move. In another second he'd have her in his arms.

Her brain kicked in, and she sidled around him and almost ran out of the bedroom up the hall to the front room. She grabbed Jeff's windbreaker and thrust it toward him when he followed her.

"Thanks for the software. And the demonstration," she said, as breathless as if she'd climbed Devil's Mountain in a sprint. "I should get to work on the program right away, before I forget."

He shrugged into his jacket. "No problem. Walk me to the front door?"

"Sure." She had to lock up after him, anyway. And the sooner he left, the better. She clattered down the stairs, not waiting to see if he followed.

Before she reached the double doors of the café, two strong hands grasped her shoulders and turned her to face him. Although the room was dark, she could read his expression in the glow from the streetlights that filtered through the display windows. His smile had disappeared, replaced by a seriousness that shook her.

"Jodie." He breathed her name like a prayer.

Gazing into the depths of eyes the color of a mountain sky just before dawn, she couldn't speak, couldn't move. All her awareness centered on the heat generated by his hands on her shoulders, burning through the thin fabric of her shirt.

"I want to kiss you," he said. "But not if you don't want me to."

She closed her eyes against the naked desire in his. He'd kissed her once before, and that brief contact had fired her blood, fueled her imagination, and made her lie awake at night, longing for him. Another kiss would only feed her burgeoning feelings for him. She didn't want to love Jeff. She'd messed up her life once before with a mere infatuation. What kind of damage would real love do?

"All you have to do is say no," he prompted with a caressing gentleness in his voice that undid all her best intentions.

She opened her eyes and met his gaze. "No."

He instantly dropped his hands from her shoulders with a sigh that wrenched her heart.

"No," she repeated. "I can't say no. I'd be lying if I did."

With a swiftness that took her breath away, he caught her in his arms, lifted her from the floor and backed her against the wall beside the door. Molding his body to hers with an intimacy that shot currents of desire from her head to toes, he claimed her mouth with his. Unable to stop herself, she wrapped her arms around his neck and wound her fingers through his hair.

Her universe contracted until only the two of them

existed, and she couldn't tell where she ended and he began. With lips parted, tongues mingling and his heart pounding against her own, she reveled in the sensation of oneness, a contradiction of peacefulness and tumult, security and danger.

Another impression, the hardness in his groin pressed against her, brought her to her senses. She broke away, drew a gasping breath and straightened her clothes with trembling hands.

He placed a hand on the wall on either side of her, forming a solid male cocoon. "Kissing you gives a whole new meaning to shock and awe."

She didn't dare look at him, afraid she'd kiss him again.

With gentle fingers, he tucked a wisp of hair behind her ear. "You okay?" he asked.

Afraid to trust her voice, she nodded.

"Sorry you didn't say no?"

"I'm…not sure." God, she sounded like a teenager. But why not? She'd been acting like an adolescent whose hormones had run amok. She finally found the courage to raise her eyes to meet his gaze.

His amazing eyes twinkled in the dim light. "Guess you'll need more chances to make up your mind."

"I don't—"

He placed his fingers against her lips, stopping her words and sending her thoughts spiraling again. "No need to decide now. We'll take things one step at a time. Just promise you'll make the poker run with me a week from Saturday.''

"I shouldn't—"

"But you will."

"Yes." After what they'd just shared, how could she refuse?

"I'm going to be pretty busy at the farm for a while," he explained.

"I understand."

"But I'll stay in touch."

She nodded. "Thank you. For the ice cream, the flowers, the software. You didn't have to—"

He cupped her face in his hands. "I wanted to."

She covered his hands with her own. "So did I."

The corresponding heat in his glance indicated he knew she referred to their kiss.

He brushed her lips lightly with his own and then opened the door. She waited until he'd mounted his cycle and roared away before locking the café and turning toward the stairs.

Brittany stood silhouetted on the top step in the light from the apartment. Jodie wondered how much her daughter had seen and heard.

When Brittany quickly disappeared and her bedroom door slammed shut, Jodie had her answer.

Chapter Nine

Jeff stared at the grant application on his computer screen but didn't see the words. Instead he pictured the luminescence of Jodie's face, her huge eyes shining like stars in the streetlight's glow after he'd kissed her three nights ago, an image that had occupied every waking hour since then.

Usually the spartan sanctuary of his farmhouse office with its bare floor of broad oak planks, battered pine desk and comfortable overstuffed furniture soothed his mind. Often after a contentious encounter with one of the teens, he'd withdraw to the room's quiet solitude to relax. But today he was wound tighter than an eight-day clock, and the familiar surroundings refused to work their usual magic. He shoved back from his desk, rose from his chair and paced.

He hadn't expected to feel this way about Jodie, hadn't intended to become so involved. With sixteen hellions to tame, a staff to supervise and a farm to run, he didn't have time for a personal life. He'd thought he would simply pass a day of R&R now and then with Jodie, but he'd been unprepared for her effect on him. She consumed his thoughts from dawn to dusk, and at night she filled his dreams. And his obsession was more than physical longing, although, heaven knew, he suffered that in spades. Rehabilitating teenage offenders was no longer enough. He wanted to share that goal and every aspect of his life with the pert, pretty, gutsy woman who had stolen his heart.

And he could think of a dozen good reasons why that wasn't going to happen.

"Taking your morning hike inside?" Gofer stood in the doorway, arms folded across his chest, his shoulder propped against the door frame.

Jeff hadn't heard his friend approach and gathered that he'd been watching awhile. Jeff halted, tossed Gofer a wry smile and pushed his fingers through his hair. "Remember what Arch taught us?"

"Arch taught us a lot of things."

Jeff rotated his desk chair to face the door and plopped into it. "The most important thing, he always said, was staying focused on the mission."

Gofer nodded. "He said focus was the only way to get the job done *and* come home alive."

"*Never* lose your focus," Jeff repeated.

"And your point is?" Gofer entered the room and straddled a chair opposite Jeff.

"I've lost my focus."

Gofer studied him a moment in silence. "Jodie Nathan?"

Jeff nodded. "I can't stop thinking about her. Even when I don't see her for days at a time."

"And that's bad?"

Jeff jumped to his feet and started pacing again. At this rate he'd wear a rut in the broad plank floor. "Archer Farm is my mission. And I can't focus on it because of her."

Gofer leaned back in his chair and followed Jeff's back-and-forth passage with his eyes. "This isn't combat."

"What?" Jeff turned and stared at his friend.

"The advice Arch gave us was for life-and-death situations. Like it or not, you're a civilian now. You're entitled to a real life."

Jeff gestured toward the dorm. "But these boys—"

"Need every minute we can give them, true. But if each man on the staff takes some personal time now and then, Archer Farm will still succeed. In fact, it will do better if the team doesn't work 24/7 and suffer burnout." Gofer leaned forward and clasped his hands between his knees. "We're no longer in combat, lieutenant, although it may feel that way at times," he added with a grin.

Jeff knew what Gofer was referring to. They'd needed three staff members to break up a fight between two of the newest arrivals last night. Kermit had suffered a split lip and Ricochet a nasty punch to the groin.

"I'm not talking about R&R now and then," Jeff admitted. "I'm thinking about commitment, about being with Jodie for the long haul."

Gofer's expression showed no surprise. "And Brittany, too?"

"Like you said before, Jodie and Brit are a package. I'd adopt Brittany, if she wanted." Only after he'd spoken the words did Jeff realize how far his dreams had gone. He loved Jodie, and he could give Brittany the father she'd never had by being the father *he'd* never had. The prospect had its appeal. And a thousand obstacles. "But the whole idea's insane."

"Insanity's my specialty," Gofer said. "Tell me more."

Jeff stopped midstride and propped a hip on top of his desk. "I can't be a good husband—and father—and run Archer Farm, too."

"Why not?"

"The Marines trained me well," Jeff admitted, "but not for family life, and not for being in two places at once."

Gofer's forehead wrinkled in thought. "Have you ever considered how having a real family living at Archer Farm might be a good example for our teens?"

Jeff snorted. "Jodie live here? Not a chance."

"You've asked her?"

He shook his head. "She has a business to run and a daughter she doesn't want within ten miles of this place. It would never work."

"Okay." Gofer stood and dusted his hands. "Then just forget it. Forget her."

"That's easy for you to say."

"Yeah, it is. I'm not in love with her."

Jeff scowled. "Is this how you counsel our boys?"

"Pretty much."

"Tell them to forget whatever problem they have?"

Gofer shrugged. "If they're unwilling to do anything about the problem, what other solution is there?"

Gofer was baiting him, but Jeff wouldn't bite. "They teach you that in shrink school?"

"I practice nondirective counseling. The client explores his problem and comes up with his own solutions. Much more effective than being told what to do. We humans are stubborn creatures. We don't like following orders."

"Odd thing for a Marine to say."

"Odd but true. That's why the military has boot camps, to drill that natural resistance out of you." Gofer walked over and clapped him on the shoulder. "Your situation is far from hopeless. There's a compromise between Archer Farm and your personal life out there somewhere. Just keep looking till you find it."

Jeff grimaced. "Or forget it."

"My words exactly." Gofer headed for the door. "Meanwhile, Trace has fried chicken and corn on the cob for dinner. Good chow always makes you feel better."

Jeff took in a deep breath, blew it out hard and followed Gofer out the door.

IN THE FADING SUMMER TWILIGHT, Jodie sat with Brynn and Merrilee on the deck behind Grant and Merrilee's home outside of town, a log cabin Grant had renovated during Merrilee's years in New York. On the pond behind the house, mist trailed like a windblown scarf above the dark, placid waters. A chorus of cicadas chirped raucously among the distant trees, and, closer to the house, lightning bugs, their phosphorescent bodies winking like tiny stars, flitted through the tall, fragrant meadow grasses.

Contemplating the peaceful scene, Jodie welcomed a loosening of the tension that had been her constant companion lately. Tension caused mainly by her stand-off with Brittany. She'd tried to talk to her daughter after Brit had witnessed her kissing Jeff, but Brittany had refused to listen, hadn't wanted to spend more than a minute in the same room with her since that night. This evening Jodie was experiencing the company of people who not only listened, but responded as well, for a change.

Grant had been called to the Bickerstaff farm to

treat a sick cow, and Jodie and Brynn were enjoying their first visit with Merrilee since her wedding.

"I couldn't believe it when Mrs. Bickerstaff called for Grant." Merrilee filled glasses with chilled white wine and handed them to Brynn and Jodie. "I thought she'd died years ago. She has to be pushing one hundred, and she's running that farm by herself."

"Joe Mauney and his son help out," Jodie said, "but, still, she's an amazing woman."

"Mom says Eileen Bickerstaff's lived at the farm alone since World War II," Merrilee said. "I can't imagine how lonely she must be."

"Forget Mrs. Bickerstaff," Brynn said. "Tell us all about the honeymoon."

Merrilee blushed a deep pink. "Longboat Key was gorgeous. Tropical, exotic, miles of white sand beaches."

Jodie had never been to Florida's west coast, only Orlando and Disney World. "You must have taken tons of pictures."

"I have two great shots of Grant," Merrilee said with obvious enthusiasm, "one of him petting a dolphin at the Mote Marine Laboratory and another with a flock of injured pelicans at the Suncoast Seabird Sanctuary. I can use them both in my book."

Merrilee glowed with happiness, and Jodie was delighted for her childhood friend. Finishing up her book of photographs of the life of a country vet, which she'd already sold on proposal, and now married to Grant, whom she'd had a crush on since middle school, why shouldn't Merrilee be happy?

Unlike Jodie, whose formerly simple but contented life had become a tangle of emotions and conflicts. Only marginally aware of Merrilee's description of Florida's beaches, restaurants and shops, Jodie sipped her wine and remembered the taste of Jeff's last kiss.

A kiss that had resulted in the silent treatment Brittany had given her this past week, in spite of Jodie's best efforts to communicate.

Yesterday Gofer had called to ask if Jodie could bring Daniel home, explaining that none of the staff could get away to pick him up. She had agreed, and Brittany and Daniel had chattered constantly on the trip through the valley. But Brittany hadn't said a word directly to her mother during the entire drive.

When Jodie had pulled into the parking place in front of the farmhouse, she'd intended to drop off Daniel and leave immediately. But the kid had shot her his eager puppy dog look. "Please, Ms. Nathan, can I show Brittany the garden we planted? It's awesome."

For the first time since leaving town, Brittany looked at her, a silent plea in her green eyes. As tight as the two teenagers had become, Daniel could have offered to show Brittany dirt, and her daughter would have jumped with excitement. With Brit already angry over her mother's involvement with Jeff, Jodie couldn't say no and alienate her further.

"Go ahead," Jodie said, "but only fifteen minutes."

Brittany was out of the car before Jodie finished speaking. Jodie rolled down the van windows and tried to relax behind the wheel while she waited. Her gaze swept the property and picked out a dozen teenagers, all wearing the farm's summer uniform of cargo shorts and olive-drab T-shirts. Gone were the hip-hop clothes and do-rags. Also gone was most of their hair. Every kid, like Daniel, sported a Marine-style buzz cut. Gone, too, was their metal porcupine look with not a piece of jewelry in sight.

Also missing were the slouched postures and sullen expressions. Each boy was working, and seemed to be enjoying it.

Jodie couldn't help being impressed. The staff had worked wonders on the terrifying yet miserable teenagers who had stumbled off the bus less than a week ago. Her gaze traveled to the farmhouse, and her heart stopped. Jeff sat on the steps next to a boy built like a meat locker. Big as he already was, the teen's huge hands and feet indicated he had more growing in store. With an earnest look, the boy talked to Jeff, who never took his eyes off the teen's face. The pair were so engrossed in conversation, Jodie doubted Jeff knew she was there, which was just as well. As soon as Brittany returned, Jodie could leave without speaking.

Not speaking to Jeff worked for her on two levels.

First, she wouldn't further antagonize Brittany, who was already bent out of shape over her mother's relationship with the handsome Marine, and second, Jodie would avoid another encounter that would only fan the flames she was hoping to extinguish.

With a sigh of relief, she noted Brittany walking toward the car. At the same time, Jeff and his companion stood. Jeff threw an arm around the boy's broad shoulders and gave him a quick clap on the back, the ubiquitous male equivalent of a same-gender hug. Then the boy set off at a trot toward the barn.

And Jeff headed straight for Jodie.

She hadn't seen or talked with him since his visit to her apartment days ago. Her heart stuttered and her stomach flip-flopped at his approach. But when she observed the scowl darkening the sharp angles of his face, she took a deep breath and grew still. Something was very wrong, and she hadn't a clue what caused his murderous look.

From the corner of her eye, Jodie saw Brittany notice Jeff and turn back toward the garden. Either her daughter was granting them privacy or didn't want to speak to him.

"I'm glad you're here," he said when he reached the car, but he didn't look glad. Far from it.

"I brought Daniel home."

He leaned down and folded his powerful forearms on the door frame. A gust of breeze enveloped her in his scent, a male essence triggering memories and responses that made her skin hot.

"We've got a problem." Jeff's thundercloud expression deepened, turning his gray eyes almost black.

"Only one? I thought you had sixteen." She'd tried for a joke, but he wasn't smiling.

"It's Mrs. Weatherstone," Jeff said.

Concern for her old friend overrode her reaction to Jeff's nearness. "What's wrong?"

Jeff grabbed the handle and wrenched open the door. "Let's walk."

Jodie glanced toward the garden, where Brittany was engrossed with Daniel, her blond head and his red one bent over a row of immature corn plants. Jodie slid from the car and fell into step beside Jeff who was stomping down the drive as if headed into battle.

"What's the matter with Mrs. Weatherstone?" Jodie asked over the crunch of gravel beneath their feet and hurried to catch up. Icy dread gripped her. Her sweet friend was old and feeble, and Jodie couldn't bear the thought of anything happening to her.

Jeff stopped abruptly and glared down at Jodie. With a shudder she noted the intensity of his anger, the lightning spark in his gray eyes, the flare of his nostrils, the hard line of his mouth. He made a formidable adversary, and, as a fighting Marine, must have struck fear in the hearts of the enemy.

"Has someone hurt her?" Jodie demanded.

"Someone's sure as hell trying." His words came out in a growl. "But he'll have to deal with me first."

If ever a man looked out for blood, Jeff fit the bill. Jodie laid her hand on his arm. "Take a deep breath and tell me about it. You don't want to endanger Archer Farm by going off half-cocked."

"You're right." Jeff inhaled deeply, his expanding chest straining the fabric of his T-shirt before he released his breath. He motioned to a log that lined the drive. "Let's sit."

They had rounded a bend in the road, out of sight of the farm and leaving them essentially alone and unobserved. But as long as Jeff remained in his current agitated state, Jodie wasn't worried about a repeat of their café kiss. Right now she was more concerned for Mrs. Weatherstone.

"You saw me talking to Jason?" Jeff asked.

"The kid built like a fire hydrant?"

Jeff nodded. "He's been working this week at Mrs. Weatherstone's, washing windows, cleaning gutters. Seems a New England antiques dealer in town has made several visits to our old friend. Jason's not an eavesdropper, but standing on a ladder with the windows open, he couldn't help hearing."

"I can understand an antiques dealer being interested in Mrs. Weatherstone." But Jodie didn't understand Jeff's anger. "That three-story house is crammed with valuable pieces."

Jeff nodded. "The guy told her that since she didn't use the second and third floors, she might as well sell off the stuff. Suggested that she donate the money to a good cause."

Jodie frowned. "And that's why you're angry?"

Jeff heaved a sigh of exasperation. "Mrs. Weatherstone has the right to do whatever she wishes with her belongings. But she doesn't deserve to be scammed."

"The man's not an antiques dealer?"

"He's some kind of wheeler-dealer, all right, according to Jason."

"You must have gained that kid's trust awfully fast. Isn't it out of character for him to rat someone out, even a stranger?"

Jeff almost smiled. "Jason doesn't trust me. He's covering his butt, afraid he might be blamed if Mrs. Weatherstone's ripped off. And I wouldn't say this to his face, but I also believe he's grown fond of the old lady. She has that effect on people."

"How did Jason know she was being cheated? Most teens aren't antiques experts."

Jeff's grin widened. "I have to give him credit. Jason used part of his supervised computer time to check out eBay. After looking at comparable items up for sale, he discovered the dealer's offering Mrs. Weatherstone less than a penny on the dollar."

Disgust at the antiques dealer's tactics consumed her. "Mrs. Weatherstone's no dummy."

Jeff shook his head. "But the man's playing on her philanthropic nature. Jason said she told the dealer about Archer Farm and how she'd donate the money from the sale of her antiques to us. Considering that she inherited most of those pieces and paid low prices by today's values for the others decades ago, she probably thinks she's being well compensated."

"And doing a good deed at the same time," Jodie agreed. "What rock did this guy crawl out from under?"

"This part of the country is ripe for the pickings," Jeff said. "Mountain folk are frugal and don't throw anything away. When I was a kid, Daddy used to run off people all the time who were just driving around, hoping to make a killing off antiques they purchased for a very small fraction of their worth."

"Let Brynn handle this," Jodie suggested. "You're too angry. You might do something you regret."

"The voice of experience?" Jeff's tone had softened, the anger had left his face, and he reached for her hand. "You're not sorry about the other night, are you?"

Jodie stood and avoided his grasp. And his question. "I'll stop by Mrs. Weatherstone's on the way home and warn her not to make a sale until she's had a certified appraisal. Do you want me to contact Brynn?"

As if to keep from reaching for her again, Jeff

shoved his hands in the back pockets of his cargo shorts. "I'll call her. She'll want to talk to Jason."

Jodie set off at a brisk stride toward her van, and Jeff walked alongside. "Thanks for filling me in."

"No problem. How's the computer program coming?" His tone was casual again.

"I'm still working out a few bugs."

"Let me know if you need help."

"Thanks." If her emotions hadn't been in such turmoil, she would have laughed at the facade they were projecting, conversing as nonchalantly as if discussing the weather, while the magnetism between them pulled with the strength of the earth holding the moon in its orbit. How could she not love a man who, every time she saw him, gave her more reasons to? His concern for Mrs. Weatherstone was one more example that proved his heart was in the right place, that he was a friend who could be trusted.

She reached the van, slid onto the driver's seat and closed the door. Jeff leaned toward her through the open window, and she had to force herself to breathe. How could one man look so gorgeous?

"We still on for the poker run?" he asked.

"I think so," she said, waffling. Unless she could find a way to weasel out. She and Jeff had no future together, so what was the point? He had Archer Farm, and she had Brittany, not exactly a dynamite combination, especially since Jodie was a total novice at love and had no clue how to handle a relationship with such overwhelming complications.

Brittany had climbed into the passenger seat then, and Jodie had headed immediately for town and Mrs. Weatherstone's.

And she hadn't spoken with Jeff since.

"Guess what?" Merrilee was saying.

"What?" Jodie forced her thoughts back to the present.

"River Walk's for sale."

"I saw the sign on my way here," Brynn said.

"Me, too," Jodie said.

The exclusive contemporary "cabin" on the river across the highway from the Stattons was where Senator Mercer and Randy had stayed that fateful summer. The sight of the For Sale sign had reminded Jodie that Brittany had been making more rumblings recently about contacting her paternal grandparents, her daughter's special method of needling Jodie with her displeasure over her mother's interest in Jeff.

"Mark my words," Brynn said, "some rich Yankee will buy the place."

"It will take someone with money," Merrilee added, and quoted the asking price.

Brynn whistled at the exorbitant sum.

"Speaking of Yankees," Jodie said to Brynn, "what's happened with the antiques dealer and Mrs. Weatherstone?"

Brynn took a sip of wine and twirled her glass by

the stem. "I found him staying at Tuttle's Bed and Breakfast. Told him I'd throw his sorry butt in jail if he didn't stop harassing old ladies. He checked out the next morning. No one's seen him since."

"Good." Jodie had warned Mrs. Weatherstone, but the old woman was naive and had found it hard to believe her antiques were worth more than the man was offering.

"How are things with you and Jeff?" Brynn asked, catching Jodie by surprise.

"Jodie and Jeff?" Merrilee's eyebrows shot upward and her sky-blue eyes lit with interest. "What's this? I leave town for a couple weeks and look what happens."

"Nothing's happened," Jodie grumbled. "Jeff gave me some computer business software, that's all."

"Not the way I hear it." Brynn considered her with wicked delight.

"Then you heard wrong," Jodie insisted.

Merrilee and Brynn were her best friends, but how could she tell them what her feelings were for Jeff, when Jodie didn't understand those emotions herself?

"You mean you're not riding in the poker run with him?" Brynn asked.

"Absolutely not," Jodie said, and meant every word. Jeff just didn't know it yet.

Chapter Ten

Heavy rains plagued the Upstate for days, but the morning of the poker run dawned clear and delightfully cool for late June. Brittany was waiting tables in the café. Sophie, who'd arrived early to fill Jodie's spot as hostess for the day, was busy seating customers. Behind the counter Maria was hustling to keep up with the steady influx of breakfast orders.

Upstairs Jodie, emotions running hot and cold, plaited her hair into a French braid and scowled at herself in the mirror. In spite of her strongest intentions not to ride with Jeff, she was preparing to do exactly that.

And it was all Brynn's aunt Marion's fault.

Right before closing, a few days ago, Jodie had picked up the phone to call Jeff and cancel, when Marion Sawyer had breezed into the café and plopped onto a stool at the counter. The tall woman with huge bones, big hair, a strong jaw and a heart as large as the rest of her, had ordered coffee and a bowl of blackberry cobbler with ice cream.

"Need to talk to you, honey bun," Marion said to Jodie with a wink.

"Sold River Walk yet?" Jodie hung up before completing her call, filled a coffee mug for the new arrival and folded her arms on the counter, while behind her, Maria heated fresh cobbler in the microwave and scooped ice cream.

Marion, who worked with her husband Bud in the real estate office three doors west of the café, was dressed to kill in a linen dress the color of ripe watermelon and a matching jacket, a sure sign she'd been showing houses. She shook her head at Jodie's question. "Need to find just the right buyer."

"Someone with a truckload of money?"

"That plus a flaming desire to get away from it all. Pleasant Valley's not big on excitement, although, Lord knows we've had enough lately." Marion blew on her coffee and took a sip.

"What excitement?" Jodie had been so wrapped up in recent worries over the café's finances, Brittany, who was still on restriction and playing the martyr to the hilt, and Jodie's unsettling feelings for Jeff, that she hadn't paid attention to the latest gossip.

"That poor Davidson boy," Marion said with a shake of her head that didn't stir a single lacquered strand in her bouffant hairdo. Her eyes were sorrowful.

Jodie's breath caught in her throat. "Something's happened to Jeff?"

"Not yet, and not if I have anything to do with it. Thanks, Maria." Marion dug her spoon into the bowl Jodie's cook had set before her and shoveled in a mouthful of the rich dessert.

Jodie puzzled over Marion's statement and was about to ask for clarification when Marion swallowed and spoke. "You riding with him on the poker run Saturday?"

"I'm—"

"Good, because we definitely need him there."

Resistance is futile, Jodie thought with a grimace and sighed. She'd watched too many *Star Trek* reruns. "Why do you need Jeff?"

"We're mounting a campaign to counteract the busybodies trying to shut down Archer Farm."

Jeff hadn't mentioned the opposition the last time they'd spoken, and Jodie, not having heard further rumblings in the café, had assumed the brouhaha and accompanying opposition to the project had died down. "I thought the poker run was to raise money for needy kids at Christmas."

Marion scooped another spoonful. "Two birds with one stone, honey bun."

"I don't understand."

Marion leaned toward her with a conspiratorial air. "Well, Agnes Tuttle has had this killer bee in her bonnet ever since Jeff came back to town. She started the petitions against the farm and is heading up the drive to boot him out. Says we don't need Jeff's kind here. Considers his boys a threat to her daughter.''

''Caroline's thirty-three years old,'' Jodie said with a sputter of surprise. ''I hardly think she'll run off with a teenage delinquent.''

Caroline was a beautiful woman whose mother kept her under her thumb and worked her almost to death, running their bed and breakfast, the only lodgings in town. Jodie recalled that in high school, and later, after Merrilee had moved to New York, Caroline had set her sights on Grant. But with Grant now happily married, Caroline seemed doomed to a life of fetching and carrying for her tyrant of a mother, especially since Mrs. Tuttle kept Caroline too busy to meet new people, except for their guests, who were merely passing through.

''When we gather at Ridge's barbecue at the end of the run,'' Marion said, ''we'll have our own petitions in favor of Archer Farm for everyone to sign.''

''Is the Chamber of Commerce supporting Jeff?'' Jodie asked. Marion's husband, Bud, was president of that august group.

Marion held one hand out palm down and waggled it one way, then the other. ''They're split almost down the middle. Some merchants fear the project will be bad for business. If folks know about it, it might scare them off from making a stop here when they're headed to and from the mountains. Others, like Bud, insist what Jeff's doing is good PR, so we can call Pleasant Valley 'the town with a heart.'"

Jodie thought of Agnes Tuttle, a mean-spirited, bitter woman, whose veins coursed with vinegar. If that woman had a heart, it was pickled in brine. Some claimed she'd henpecked her poor husband to death decades ago. Although almost universally unpopular, Agnes was likely to draw folks to her side. No one wanted the old battle-ax as an enemy who'd go out of her way to make their lives miserable. Agnes was a formidable opponent, even for a Marine who'd survived combat overseas.

"We've invited everyone who'll come, not just the riders, to meet at Ridge's barbecue after the run," Marion said. "The bigger show of support, the better chance of defeating Agnes and her crowd. I'm counting on you to help circulate the petitions."

"You'll have plenty of folks for that. You won't need me." Jodie was sure Jeff would still participate in the run without her, especially if she told him about the postrun meeting to sign supportive petitions.

Marion frowned and fixed Jodie with a probing stare. "I didn't think you'd object. You hired one of Jeff's boys, didn't you?"

Jodie nodded. "Daniel's a good worker."

"Then what's the problem?"

Jodie refilled Marion's cup and avoided her gaze. Jeff had his farm, and, even if he hadn't, Brittany had demonstrated clearly that she considered any man in her mother's life a threat. Jodie was falling in love with Jeff, but felt too vulnerable to follow her heart. She was terrified of making another mistake, of being the wrong woman for Jeff, of alienating Brittany, of screwing up her boring but peaceful life. Jodie didn't need to be involved in Jeff's fight. Marion and her friends would prevail over Agnes Tuttle without Jodie's help.

And who stood up for you when you needed help? her conscience prodded. Memories flooded Jodie of the people in town who'd reached out to her when she'd been a lonely, pregnant teenager and, later, who'd flocked to her café when she first opened her doors and were good customers to this day. These same good folks were trying to help Jeff keep Archer Farm. How could Jodie not join their fight?

"I don't have a problem," Jodie assured Marion, hoping she wouldn't regret her words.

"Then you're in, honey bun?"

With a sigh of resignation, Jodie had tossed Marion a weak smile and conceded, hoping she wouldn't regret her decision. "I'm in."

"In over my head and sinking fast," Jodie admitted to her reflection in her bathroom mirror as she completed braiding her hair. Not that she minded supporting Archer Farm. She just wished she could endorse Jeff's project in a less intimate fashion than spending the day with her arms wrapped around the man she was trying hard not to love.

JEFF SAT ASTRIDE his Harley and watched Jodie stroll toward him along the sidewalk. Just looking at her made his chest tighten, as if a phantom fist squeezed his heart. Wearing snug jeans, a white turtleneck, an embroidered denim jacket and high-heeled boots that elevated her petite stature to almost five foot five, she was a walking dream. When she tossed her head, flinging an errant curl away from her face, sunlight glinted in her eyes with their intriguing mix of green and brown that reminded him of spring leaves against willow bark.

He slid off his bike and jammed his hands in the pockets of his old leather jacket to keep from reaching for her. "Hey."

"Hey, yourself." She eyed his cycle with obvious trepidation. "I'm not sure I can stay on that thing."

"Just hang on to me and you'll be fine." He reached onto the rear seat and unfastened his new leather jacket and extra helmet. "But you'll need these."

"I have a jacket," she protested.

"Denim won't protect you against wind chill." He held up the leather garment.

Jodie slipped her arms into the sleeves and almost disappeared into the too-big jacket. Its hem hit her below the hip. She raised her arms to her sides, her hands lost in the long sleeves. "It's huge!"

"The more it covers, the warmer you'll be." Jeff folded the sleeves back to expose her hands, zipped the jacket to her chin and resisted the urge to enfold her, jacket and all, in his arms. "Now for the helmet."

"I'll do it." Jodie took the headgear from him, jammed it on and threw him a crooked grin. "I'm ready for my close-up now, Mr. DeMille."

"You look—" He'd started to say "great," but at the cool glance she shot him, he amended it to "all set."

"No one will mistake me for a biker babe in this getup," she said with a laugh. "Shoot, they can't even tell I'm female."

"I don't think that's a problem," Jeff admitted in the understatement of the year. Anyone not legally blind would note the seductive curve of her calves, the trimness of her ankles, and the delicacy of her hands. Jodie was unmistakably one hundred percent woman, and if he didn't mount his bike soon, she'd observe his body attesting to that fact.

He swung onto the seat, steadied her with his arm as she climbed behind him and kick-started the engine. "Lower your visor to protect your eyes," he shouted above the Harley's roar. "And hold on tight."

With Jodie clinging to him, he eased the powerful cycle slowly through town and opened it wide on the highway. The verdant beauty of the countryside in summer, the rush of chilly mountain air on his face and the warmth of Jodie, spooned against his back and legs, were a heady combination. With his teen-agers settling in at the farm and the team functioning like a well-oiled machine, he should have felt that all was right with his world.

But there was one major glitch.

Since his talk with Gofer, Jeff had lain awake nights trying to think of a compromise that would work for him and Jodie. And for all his efforts, he had come up with zilch. But he hadn't thrown in the towel yet. And the pressure of Jodie's arms around his waist and the heat of her legs against his urged him to enjoy the day and worry about the future later.

Across the North Carolina line at Cashiers, he pulled into a convenience store, where the first draw was scheduled. After he and Jodie had each selected a card from the deck held by one of the ride volun-teers set up at a card table near the door, he went inside and bought huge cups of coffee.

Jodie stripped off the leather jacket and helmet and accepted the drink with a pinched look.

"Something wrong?" he asked.

"I'm a little stiff," she admitted.

He should have realized that gripping a cycle on winding mountain curves flexed muscles Jodie didn't use often.

"Let's walk to limber up," he said. "We made good time, so there's no hurry."

They crossed the intersection to a farmers market on the corner and wandered among the stands of fresh vegetable and flowers, bags of boiled peanuts, and jars of sourwood honey. The shops that lined the highways were packed with tourists, and within a few minutes Jeff spotted car license tags from eight different states.

"Feeling better?" he asked.

Jodie nodded. "I just needed to work out the kinks."

"If you're not up to the rest of the ride, I can take you back now." The last thing he wanted was to interrupt their day together, but he didn't want her uncomfortable, either.

"I'll be fine." She gazed up at him, eyes shining in the sunlight, that same flyaway curl dangling over her eye.

He tucked the lock behind her ear and ran his knuckles down the silky smoothness of her cheek. "You're doing great. Sure you've never ridden before?"

"You'd be surprised at all the things I've never done before." Regret weighted her tone.

"You should make a list," he suggested, "of everything you want to try. Then do them and check them off one by one."

Her answering smile was crooked and twisted his heart. "And who'd raise my child and run my business while I'm running through my list?"

"Don't think of it as a list. Pick one thing at a

time. Say, one a week. At the end of a year, you can look back on over fifty new experiences you've had.''

She shook her head sadly. ''You make it sound so easy.''

He thrust his empty coffee cup into a nearby trash receptacle, grasped her by the shoulders and gazed into her eyes. ''What's easier is not trying, living exactly the same from day to day. Until you're old enough to realize that life has passed you by and you haven't done the things you wanted. Accepting that fact won't be easy.''

His own words jolted him. He wanted to live his life with Jodie, wanted to share those new experiences with her, wanted to look back with her in their old age on a life spent together.

''What would be the first thing on your list?'' he asked.

''Dancing,'' she replied instantly. ''Before Brittany, I loved to dance.''

He couldn't help grinning. ''Your wish is my command. Let's go.''

He turned her toward the convenience store, grabbed her hand and hurried her along.

''Where?'' she asked.

''To finish the poker run. There's a jukebox at Ridge's. We've got some dancing to do.''

''But...'' She stopped short and dug in her heels.

''But what?''

"It's been fifteen years." Her face flushed. "I don't remember how."

"It's like riding a bicycle. It'll all come back to you." Hell, he hoped so. The last time he'd danced had been at a honky-tonk outside the Parris Island Marine Base over a decade ago. But he'd risk looking like an idiot for the chance to hold her in his arms.

"And when you're too tired to dance," he added, "we'll find us a quiet table and make the rest of your list."

"Only if you make one, too," she insisted.

"Oh, yeah," he agreed. And he knew exactly how he'd fill in the number-one slot.

WHEN JEFF PARKED his Harley in front of the darkened café later that night and gave Jodie a hand to dismount, she wished their day together could have lasted forever. For a few brief hours she'd forgotten the demands of her business, the responsibilities of parenthood. And she'd felt like a teenager again.

After the first stop, she'd relaxed a bit, so her muscles hadn't cramped as badly after that, and she'd enjoyed the journey along the narrow mountain highways with sunlight dappling the roads through the thick summer foliage of the overhanging trees. The best part of the ride, however, had been snuggling against Jeff, the steady rhythm of his pulse beneath her palms, the heat of his body mingling with hers, and his heady scent that enveloped her from his proximity—and his borrowed jacket.

Once they'd reached Ridge's, they'd gorged themselves on the Upstate's best barbecue, coleslaw and French fries. Then Bud Sawyer had tapped his spoon against a glass for quiet and requested everyone to sign the petitions in support of Archer Farm. By the time the winning poker hand was announced, Bud had over one hundred signatures, even if a few were stained with Ridge's famous barbecue sauce. The petition support had pleased Jodie, until Jeff confided that Agnes Tuttle had already collected three times that many.

With a full house Brynn had drawn along the route, she held the winning poker hand and donated her cash prize to the children's Christmas fund. But she and the officer from Walhalla had shifts to work, so they left immediately after eating.

The rest of the crowd slowly drifted away, but Jeff had shown no eagerness to depart. Instead he'd fed a handful of change into the jukebox and drawn Jodie into his arms. Time had stood still as they'd slow danced around the cramped wooden dance floor at the back of the restaurant. The supper crowd disappeared, the bar filled with its Saturday night regulars, and still Jodie and Jeff danced. Between the blaring music and the noise of the crowd, they couldn't have heard each other speak, but Jodie had no desire for talk. All she wanted was for Jeff to hold her and the music to last forever.

The music made her recall that her mother and father loved Anne Murray and played her songs often at home. The lyrics from one favorite ran through Jodie's mind as Jeff guided her expertly around the floor.

Can I have this dance for the rest of my life...

A glance at the clock above the bar brought her back to reality. Her mother was staying with Brittany, and Jodie didn't want to keep Sophie up late.

"I have to go," she shouted above the din.

Jeff hadn't protested, although the heat in his eyes threatened to dissolve her where she stood. He bundled her into the jacket and helmet again, and they roared into the night with the Harley's headlight cutting through the darkness like a shining blade.

In front of the café, Jodie removed the helmet, shrugged off Jeff's jacket and handed them to him. "I had a wonderful time."

"We didn't get around to making your list," Jeff said. "There's still time tonight." He glanced up to her apartment, where lights shone in Brittany's windows.

"I'll have to pass on the list." A worry that Jodie had tucked into the back of her mind resurfaced with a vengeance. "But I would like your advice on the software you gave me."

Jeff removed his helmet and hooked it over the handlebar. "Having problems?"

"I'll say." But Jodie wasn't sure the difficulty lay in the computer program. She hoped Jeff could prove her wrong.

She led the way upstairs, and Jeff followed.

Sophie greeted them and hurried to depart. "I have cookies to bake for fellowship hour at church tomorrow," she explained.

In Jodie's bedroom, Jeff sat at the computer and called up the financial reports for the café.

"I've been over these countless times, and I've worked them out on paper, too," she explained. "No matter what I do, I can't reconcile the figures."

Jeff concentrated on the screen and after checking and rechecking, he turned to Jodie with a frown. "You're more than six hundred dollars short."

"Damn." Jodie sank onto her bed, a sick feeling in the pit of her stomach. "I was hoping I'd miscalculated."

Jeff shook his head. "Any idea where it went?"

Jodie blew out a deep breath. "There's only one explanation. Someone's stealing from the register."

"This ever happened before?"

"Never."

"Any suspects?"

Jodie shook her head, and a thought hit her, one she didn't want to contemplate because it only increased the queasiness in her stomach.

Jeff must have seen the distress in her eyes. "What?"

"There is one coincidence. The shortages began the day after Daniel started work."

At the sound of a strangled cry, she turned toward the door. Brittany stood on the threshold, and the look she threw her mother was withering. Before Jodie could speak, Brittany rushed into her room and slammed the door with a force that made the windows rattle.

Chapter Eleven

Sundays at the café were a madhouse.

Tourists flocked in early on the way to spend a day in the mountains. By the time the travelers were thinning, early church services ended and locals flooded the restaurant. By four o'clock, when Jodie closed for the day, she was beat. The fact that she'd lain awake the previous night, reliving her incredible day with Jeff and the unforgettable good-night kiss they'd shared, and also worrying over the missing money, added to her exhaustion.

The last customer had paid his tab and gone. Maria and the wait staff had left, too, but Jodie was too weary to rise from the chair where she'd finally collapsed to lock the door and hang the Closed sign.

The bell over the front entry tinkled, and Jodie glanced up to see Jeff enter. She was tired, but not so worn-out that her pulse rate didn't leap into hyperdrive at the sight of him, vividly reviving the memory of last night's farewell embrace.

Today, in the Archer Farm uniform of cargo shorts, work boots and olive-drab T-shirt, he looked so good, she wanted to fling herself at him.

Fortunately, she didn't have the energy.

"Hey," he greeted her. "Busy day?"

"A hundred months of Sundays like this and I can retire," she said with a tired grin.

"Daniel here?"

Jodie glanced around. "No. He's not out front?"

Jeff shook his head. "He always waits there. I thought he might be working late."

Jodie pushed to her feet. "I'll check the deck. Maybe he and Brittany are out there."

Within seconds she returned. "No sign of them out back. I'll look upstairs."

"This isn't like Daniel." Concern added a harshness to Jeff's voice, and a frown etched the rugged angles of his face. "He's always where he's supposed to be when he's supposed to be."

"He's a teenager," Jodie reminded him with a smile. "And easily distracted, especially by Brittany."

But she wasn't smiling when she clattered down the stairs a moment later, grasping a sheet of her daughter's lavender notebook paper that had been folded, addressed to her and propped on the kitchen island.

"Daniel didn't steal the money," Brittany had

written in her looping, immature script. "We're leaving to find someone who cares."

"They're gone," she told Jeff.

His eyebrows knotted in puzzlement as he read the note. "Where?"

For months Jodie had witnessed Brittany's alienation and building resentment, helpless to defuse them, and wondered when the looming crisis would occur. She'd feared it was only a matter of time before her daughter took out her pique at Jodie by attempting to contact her paternal grandparents again. Brittany had constructed a fairy-tale image of the Mercers as the perfect grandparents, who would welcome her with open arms, side with her against her overbearing, didn't-have-a-clue mother, and allow the teen total freedom. Although Jodie had tried to provide a realistic picture of the senator and his wife, Brit refused to believe her.

Guilt racked Jodie. She should have stayed at home Saturday and tried another heart-to-heart talk with Brittany instead of dancing the night away with Jeff like a fool with no responsibilities. She was a mother, first and foremost.

And she'd blown it, big-time. Now Brittany had run away.

Jodie pushed her fingers through her hair and tried to order her swirling thoughts. "Brittany overheard us talking about the missing money last night. She must have assumed we were going to charge Daniel and convinced him to run away with her."

Jeff muttered a curse beneath his breath. "Everyone's innocent until proven guilty. I had planned to sit down with him this afternoon to find out what he knows."

He strode toward the front door, took out his cell phone and made a hurried call. Jodie couldn't help overhearing his conversation with Gofer, advising the psychologist and the rest of the staff to be on the lookout for Daniel and Brit, in case they had headed toward the farm.

Jeff ended his call and turned back to Jodie. "I have to find Daniel. Fast. If he's caught violating parole, he'll be sent to adult prison."

Already panicked over Brittany, Jodie shivered with revulsion at the knowledge of what prison would wreak on a sensitive kid like Daniel.

"Any idea where they've gone?" Jeff asked.

"Columbia's my best guess. Brittany's under the illusion that her grandfather, the senator, gives a damn. I'm sure she thinks he'll help them."

"Will he?"

Jodie scowled. "I doubt he'll even speak to her. He'll probably call the police, which definitely won't help Daniel."

"How long have they been gone?"

Jodie tried to remember when she'd last seen Brittany or Daniel earlier that afternoon. "Maybe an hour. Maybe less."

Jodie thanked God Jeff was with her. She was too tired to think straight. And too frightened for her daughter to handle this alone. A sudden clap of thunder shook the building, and the skies opened again, resuming the heavy rains that had saturated the area the previous week. Weather reports were forecasting floods if the deluge didn't ease soon.

"We'll be soaked on the Harley," Jeff said. "Can we take your van?"

Jodie nodded, followed him out of the café and locked the doors.

"I'll drive," Jeff offered.

Without protest, Jodie tossed him the keys. Between exhaustion and worry over Brittany, she'd be an accident waiting to happen if she drove.

As soon as they had entered the van and fastened their seat belts, Jeff handed her his car phone. "Better alert your parents. If the kids haven't left town, they might go to your folks. And call Brynn."

"She'll involve the police—"

"That's a chance we have to take. Is there a bus out of town today?"

"The last one left at noon."

Jeff backed the van into the street, headed east, and switched on the wipers at their highest speed against the torrential downpour. "Then they're probably hitchhiking."

Icy fear gripped Jodie at the thought of her beautiful but naive daughter climbing into a stranger's car. And Daniel, bless his sweet boyish heart, even more of an innocent than Brittany, would be as much a target as her daughter.

"Unless Jodie has any friends who might give them a ride?" Jeff added.

Jodie shook her head. "Only old pals at Carsons Corner, and they'd have to steal another car. None of them is old enough to drive."

"Daniel wouldn't go for car theft," Jeff said. "He knows he'd be locked up for certain."

"But he ran away."

Jeff shrugged. "Brittany must have convinced him you were going to charge him with theft." He shot her a piercing gaze before returning his attention to the rain-slicked road. "Were you?"

Jodie shook her head. "I intended to dump the whole problem in Brynn's lap."

"Anyone else on your staff you suspect?"

"No one. But I don't know them all that well. Maria and a couple of the waitresses haven't worked for me but a few months."

"So anyone could have used Daniel's arrival to cover his or her tracks, hoping the blame would fall on the resident delinquent?"

"I suppose." She peered through the rain. "Where are we going?"

"We'll take the fastest route to Columbia, via

I-26,'' Jeff explained. ''We'll check major exits and rest areas along the way.'' He reached over and squeezed her hand. ''Now make your calls.''

JEFF CONCENTRATED on the road and silently cursed the weather. A tropical system had hit the Louisiana coast as a hurricane, weakened into a rainmaker, slowly worked its way inland and stalled, dumping inches of water on ground already too saturated to absorb more. With limited visibility, conditions for a search couldn't be much worse. The kids could be standing on the shoulder of the highway, thumbing a ride, and he wouldn't see them through the downpour.

Beside him, Jodie completed calls to her parents and Brynn and returned his cell phone. Jeff had to give her credit. She'd kept her words calm, rational. If he hadn't noted her pallor, the panic in her hazel eyes, and the tremor in her hands, he wouldn't have guessed how frantic she was from her tone of voice.

''Mom and Dad are organizing a search in town,'' Jodie said, ''and Brynn's issuing an all-points bulletin, omitting the fact that Daniel's violating parole. She's hoping the Highway Patrol will spot them. She's also alerting the Columbia Police Department.''

Her composure broke then, and she swallowed a sob.

Jeff reached for her, squeezed her fingers hard, and released her. He wanted to hang on, but the slick road conditions required both hands on the wheel. "We'll find them."

"How can you sound so sure?"

"You know your daughter. If you think she's headed for the senator, I'm betting that's exactly where she'll be."

"What if I'm wrong? Or worse, what if someone…"

"Stop," he ordered. "Don't torture yourself by thinking the worst. We'll find her."

"This is all my fault."

"You can't blame yourself."

"But Brittany blames me."

"For what?"

"Where should I begin?" Irony laced Jodie's words. "For not giving her a father, for alienating her paternal grandparents, for suspecting Daniel, for falling in love—"

She'd clamped her lips shut, and from the corner of his eye, Jeff noted color flooding back into her face. She'd never admitted loving him, but he'd held on to that hope. He'd also tried making friends with Brittany, hoping to win her approval for his relationship with her mother. Apparently, he'd failed.

"Is Brittany jealous?" he asked.

"Her whole life, it's always been just the two of us. The thought of anyone intruding into our private world frightens her. She's a complicated kid. She's reached the stage where she doesn't want me telling her what to do, and another grown-up in her life would only compound her problem." Jodie sighed. "And she's afraid that if I love someone else, I'll love her less."

"Do you love someone else?" Jeff held his breath for the answer. The swish and thump of the windshield wipers and the pummeling rain on the van's roof filled the silence.

To his regret, Jodie finally shook her head. "What would be the point?"

Jeff hid his disappointment. "Does love need a reason?"

"Maybe not," Jodie said with an irritated toss of her head, "but it doesn't mean abandoning common sense, either."

"Meaning?"

"I have more than enough to juggle as my life is now. Love's a luxury I can't afford."

"Having a daughter and a business doesn't mean you're not entitled to a life of your own," he argued, recognizing that he'd voiced similar concerns about his own life to Gofer not long ago. Archer Farm was his mission, Brittany was Jodie's. And Jeff had yet to find the compromises Gofer insisted were there.

"Obviously, I can't do it all," Jodie said, reinforcing Jeff's thoughts. "If I were a better mom, Brittany wouldn't have run away."

Jeff wished for the right words to convince Jodie to quit beating up on herself. "I've learned a lot from

Gofer. Teenagers are complex. Relationships are complex. Life is complex."

Jodie issued a snort that sounded like disdain. "You don't have to be a psychologist to know that, just alive and breathing."

"But that's not all Gofer's taught me," Jeff said. "I've learned that for every chance to screw things up, there's an opportunity to make things right. I wouldn't have started Archer Farm if I didn't believe that. And Brittany has far more going for her than any of my teens."

He could feel Jodie staring at him but kept his eyes on the road.

"She has a mom who loves her," Jeff continued, "a wonderful extended family, a stable home environment, a caring community—"

"Then why is she running away?" Jodie wailed.

"When we find her, you can ask her."

But finding Brittany was easier said than done. In the relentless pelting rain, they checked convenience stores at exits and rest rooms at rest stops, but found no sign of the teens or anyone who'd seen them.

By the time Jeff and Jodie reached the outskirts of Columbia, darkness had fallen. Their clothes were damp, Jodie's face was pinched with exhaustion, and Jeff's back ached between his shoulder blades from too many tense hours behind the wheel.

He pulled off at the next exit and headed toward the bright lights of a restaurant. "You need to eat."

"I'm not hungry," Jodie said. "Let's keep looking."

"You have an address for the senator?"

She shook her head.

"Then we can grab a bite while we check the phone book."

AT THE RESTAURANT, Jodie had shoved her untouched plate aside. How could she eat when she had no idea where her daughter was? Brittany could be huddled anywhere, soaked, hungry and frightened but too stubborn to call home.

The restaurant telephone directory had yielded only the address of the senator's downtown office, closed until nine o'clock the next morning, according to the recorded message on his voice mail. His home phone was unlisted, and, despite Jodie's pleas, the Information operator had refused to divulge it or the home address.

"It's probably no consolation," Jeff said once they'd climbed back into the van, "but if we can't find the senator, Brit and Daniel can't, either. They'll probably wait until morning and try his office."

"She's only fourteen. She shouldn't be out there alone, especially not this late and in this weather."

Jodie's panic amplified by the minute. She no longer felt certain that Brittany had headed for Columbia. What if she and Daniel had concocted some crazy scheme to run away to California. Or Alaska? Or God-knew-where?

Jodie took a deep breath, released it and forced herself to think. The note had stated the teens would find someone who cared, a tip-off to Brit's fantasy about her paternal grandparents. With her grandfather Mercer a powerful senator, Brit probably believed he could fix anything. Even theft charges against Daniel. Jodie had to continue this avenue of searching.

"Let's check the bus stations," she suggested. "The YMCA. Buildings around the senator's office. Maybe the kids will choose a spot like those to keep dry until morning."

For an instant Jeff looked ready to protest, but instead put the van in drive and pulled onto the highway and headed for the core of the city.

Hours later Jodie still had found no trace of Brittany. She lay back against the headrest and closed her eyes. She was living a parent's worst nightmare and couldn't wake up.

"You need sleep," Jeff said before starting the engine after their last stop. "There was a Hampton Inn at the last exit."

"I can't sleep, not knowing where Brit is."

Jeff's phone rang in the darkness. Jodie glanced at the clock on the dashboard, and her heart stopped. A call at 2:00 a.m. was seldom good news. Jeff answered the phone, then passed it to Jodie. "It's your mom."

"Mama?" Her heart pounded in her chest like a tennis shoe banging in a clothes dryer, and she braced herself for bad news.

"They're safe," Sophie said instantly, ending Jodie's agony. "Brittany and Daniel are here with us."

Jodie sat up upright. Relief cascaded through her like a cool drink on a hot day. "They never left home?"

"They left all right," Sophie said. "They've been to Columbia and back."

Anger tainted the satisfaction of Jodie's relief. "We've been scouring the city for them."

"Brittany says she found the senator's home address last week in some of my old papers," her mother explained. "I'm sorry, Jodie. I forgot I even had that information or I'd have given it to you. Anyway, Brit and Daniel caught a ride with a trucker and went straight to the Senator's when they left the café."

"Then how did they end up back in Pleasant Valley so fast?"

"The—" Sophie uttered a scathing term, a word Jodie had never heard cross her mother's lips "—wouldn't even let those poor children in out of the rain. He called the Columbia police, who picked them up and contacted our department. Chief Sawyer pulled a few strings, and a highway patrol trooper brought them home."

"And Brittany's okay?" Jodie asked.

"Disillusioned about the senator," Sophie explained, "but otherwise she's just worn-out. I made her take a hot shower, gave her a pair of my pajamas and put her to bed in the guest room. She's sound asleep now."

"And Daniel?"

"The man called Gofer from Archer Farm picked him up. The boy seems no worse for wear, either."

"Thank God." Jodie fell back against the seat.

"You sound exhausted, dear. You should get some sleep before heading home. I don't want to worry about you and Jeff having an accident, sleepy and driving in the dark in this wretched weather."

"Tell Brittany I'll talk to her tomorrow. And thanks, Mama."

Jodie ended the call and filled Jeff in on her mother's side of the conversation.

"Poor Brittany," Jeff said. "The senator's a piece of work, calling the police on his own grandchild." He uttered a few choice curses that made Sophie's description of the politician bland by comparison.

"I tried to make Brittany understand," Jodie said. "Randy had come to Pleasant Valley that summer to try to get to know his father better. But the senator spent the entire time on the phone with calls from lobbyists and constituents. Randy could never get the senator's attention, either. That's probably why the boy drank so heavily. His old man always cared more about his political career than his own family. But

Brittany wouldn't believe me. I need to go to her,'' Jodie said.

"Your mother was right." Jeff spoke with a gentleness braced with steel. "We're both exhausted and the weather's growing worse by the minute. Flood warnings are up all over the state. We'll check into the Hampton for a few hours' sleep. Driving home will be safer in daylight, even if the rain hasn't stopped."

Although her body ached with fatigue, the euphoria of having Brittany safe after so much worry hit Jodie's system like amphetamines. "I don't think I can relax."

"I have a few remedies for that."

She did, too, and the one at the top of the list made her knees weak. She tried to think of a good reason to keep driving, but her wits failed her. Brittany was safe and asleep, the weather was horrible, and she and Jeff were too tired to continue.

She struggled to mumble, "Separate rooms," when Jeff left the car to check in.

It was almost three o'clock, and her only hope was that the motel was full for the night. Or worse, she thought with alarm, as happened in all the romantic books and movies in her experience, the Hampton would have only one room left, which she and Jeff would have to share. No way was she trusting herself to spend the night in the same room with a man who made her heart flutter, her knees wobble, and her body ache for his touch. She'd learned her lesson well from Randy Mercer. Sex without commitment was as bad a combination as gasoline and matches. A recipe for destruction.

The automatic doors of the motel entrance slid open and Jeff appeared. As he walked toward her, Jodie noted the proud carriage of his posture, the sureness of his stride, the firm determination in the set of his jaw. The man was amazing. He'd knocked himself out for almost twelve hours in the search for Daniel and Brittany, neither of whom was his own child, with never a word of complaint or loss of hope. Jodie would have collapsed under the strain without his steady support. She'd have surely wrecked the car if she'd tried the hunt alone in her frantic state of mind.

A good man.

That's what Grant had called Jeff. And that's exactly what he was. A man who, despite his own tortured childhood, had devoted himself to children society had let slip through the cracks. A man who had risked his life to serve his country with honor. A man who had stood by Jodie when she needed him most.

And Jeff was no Randy Mercer, no gangly adolescent boy struggling to prove his manhood. Jeff was the epitome of all things masculine, from his physical strength and mouthwatering good looks to his protective instincts toward women and children to his status as the ultimate warrior, a United States Marine.

How could she not love him? She didn't have a chance.

He slid into the van, moved it to a nearby parking space and handed her a key card. In spite of her earlier worries, she was disappointed that he held another key, to his own room.

They made a run for the entrance through the rain, crossed the lobby and entered the elevator. On the third floor Jeff stopped in front of her room, across the hall from his.

She slid her card into the lock, opened the door and turned to him. "I don't know how to thank you."

"This will do." Before she could react, he pulled her into his arms and lowered his lips to hers.

Chapter Twelve

Jeff awoke with his face buried in Jodie's magnolia-scented hair, her back spooned against him, his arm encircling her. He inhaled the light fragrance and held it, not wanting to let her or even the scent of her go.

He'd meant only to kiss her good-night, but when her supple body had arched against him, and her soft lips had yielded to his, reason and discipline had failed. He'd swooped her into his arms, kicked the door closed and carried her to the king-size bed.

With desire he couldn't rationalize away or resist, he'd tugged off her clothes with the desperation of a man dying of thirst seeking water. Caught in his frenzy, Jodie had helped him undress, the fire in her hazel eyes and her sweet smile urging him on, burning away all conscious thought.

Sprawled beneath him on the oversize bed, the warmth of her soft, bare skin against him, their arms and legs entwined, she'd hesitated only once.

"There's something you should know." Her face

flushed with an endearing mixture of innocence, shyness and desire.

He nuzzled his lips against the pulse throbbing in her neck. "I want to know everything about you."

She moaned softly at his touch and twisted her fingers through his hair. "If you keep that up, I won't be able to talk."

He'd lifted himself on his elbows and gazed into her eyes. "You haven't changed your mind about this?"

With a fervor that gripped him at the deepest level, he hoped not, but he wouldn't force himself on her. If she wasn't one hundred percent willing, he'd reluctantly settle for a cold shower and his own room. He loved her too much to do anything she didn't want.

Jodie shook her head but lowered her eyes, as if afraid to face him. Long, dark lashes fluttered against her flushed cheeks, sending another current of longing through him like an electric shock.

"You can tell me," he encouraged softly. "I'm listening."

She opened her eyes wide, and the green-brown swirls drew him in like a whirlpool that reached to the bottom of her soul.

"I've only done this once," she admitted with a hesitancy that twisted his heart.

"Gone to a motel with a man?" he asked.

She shook her head but kept her gaze locked on his as if braced for rejection. "Made love."

"Ah, Jodie." In his heart, he cursed Randy Mercer, who'd stolen her innocence and her confidence.

"Ridiculous, isn't it," she said with a wry smile.

He wrapped his arms around her, rolled onto his back, and pulled her gently on top of him. "Not ridiculous. It's wonderful."

She tossed her hair out of her eyes and looked at him in astonishment. "Why wonderful? I'm totally inexperienced, inept—"

"—and completely mine." He cupped her face in his hands. "This isn't about skill or experience. I love you, Jodie, and as long as you love me, everything will be all right."

He'd held his breath, waiting for her answer. The only sounds in the tastefully decorated room were the wind shrieking outside the window and the rain spattering on the panes.

"I love you, Jeff." He strained to hear her words above the howl of the storm, although the anguish in her eyes was clearly evident. "But love alone won't do us any good. You have your work. I have Brittany and my business. We're on separate paths, and, for the life of me, I can't find an intersection."

He couldn't dispute her. He'd had the same running argument in his head almost from the day he'd first walked into her café.

"Then let's take tonight," he begged, "and not worry about tomorrow."

Unexpectedly she giggled. "We'll always have Paris."

For a moment he thought she'd lost her mind.

"Sorry," she said with a shake of her head. "It's a line from *Casablanca*. Grant's an old movie buff, and I've watched too many classics with him. The old dialogue hops into my head at the strangest times."

Her expression sobered, and she continued. "But you and I are like Bogart and Bergman. Duty pulls us in separate directions."

"Not tonight," he said.

The happiness that flared in her eyes almost undid him. "No, not tonight."

They made love with an intensity and ease that belied her inexperience, that made him feel as if he'd loved her a thousand times before and wanted to several thousand times again. Exhausted, they'd fallen instantly asleep. A short time later, in a fugue state, between waking and sleeping, they'd come together again, slowly and with a tenderness that Jeff had never known.

Now, with gray light of morning seeping around the edges of the draperies, he watched Jodie asleep in his arms and knew without a doubt that he wanted to wake up every morning to her face on the pillow beside him.

The ringing of the phone brought him out of his

reverie. He reached for his cell on the bedside table and answered, noting from the digital readout on the bedside clock that it was almost 8:00 a.m.

"Jodie." He shook her gently. "It's for you. It's Brynn."

Jodie was instantly awake. She sat upright and grabbed the phone. "Hey, Brynn. Something wrong?"

She was quiet for a moment, then muttered, "Oh, no."

Jeff sat up and wrapped his arms around her. She'd already been through so much, and he could tell from her voice and expression that Brynn's news wasn't good.

After several long minutes, she spoke again. "No, not yet. Let me talk to her first."

More trouble with Brittany? Jeff wondered. But he couldn't ask. Jodie was still concentrating hard on whatever Brynn was saying.

"Thanks, Brynn. We'll be home as soon as possible."

Jodie ended the call and handed him the phone. She scrambled out of bed and reached for her clothes. "We have to hurry."

Jeff didn't argue. As much as he wanted to coax Jodie back to bed and love her one more time, her frantic urgency spurred him to dress quickly. "What's up?"

"Maria Ortega's at the police station. When she

came to work this morning and found out about Brittany and Daniel, she went straight to Brynn and confessed.''

''Maria stole the money from the register?''

Jodie yanked on her slacks, zipped them and tugged on her matching sweater. ''Her baby's been sick and she couldn't afford the medicine. She'd hoped to pay the money back before I missed it. I told Brynn I wouldn't press charges.''

''So Daniel's cleared?''

Jodie nodded, but the grimness in her expression sent a sudden chill through him. ''The theft is the least of my worries now.''

She rummaged in her purse, extracted a brush and drew it briskly through her tousled hair. Thrusting aside memories of his fingers in her soft tresses, he reached for his shoes.

''The river's rising,'' Jodie rammed the brush back into her purse. ''It's already at flood stage and expected to crest fifteen feet above that before noon tomorrow.''

Jeff threw open the draperies and glanced outside. Torrential rain had made a lake of the parking lot, and the deluge showed no signs of abating. He recalled a similar storm twenty years earlier that had sent the Piedmont River, paralleling Pleasant Valley's main street, over its banks. Mr. Weatherstone had been almost crazy worrying that the waters would continue rising and flood his shop.

The shop that was now Jodie's café.

His heart ached for her. She'd been through too much already, and now this, a force of nature that even the best of his Marine training couldn't stop. "You ready?"

She nodded. "Let's go."

They hurried through checkout and raced through the storm to the car. With the wipers working at maximum speed and water spraying from the wheels like the wake of a boat, Jeff drove onto the interstate and headed west, praying that the heavens would clear before the river swelled and flooded downtown.

JODIE FORCED the protesting muscles in her legs to make one more trip to the apartment upstairs. With the help of Brittany and the wait staff, she'd moved everything possible, gift shop inventory, furniture, and pantry supplies, to the second floor in an attempt to save it from the steadily rising water that already swirled dangerously near the pillars of the rear deck.

She descended the stairs and found Brittany on the deck, staring at the raging water through the rain-spattered glass enclosure. Grant and Merrilee were next door, helping Jodie's mother and father carry the contents of his hardware business to the second-floor storeroom.

Up and down Piedmont Avenue, merchants were scurrying to protect what they could from the coming flood. Blalock's Grocery, Bud and Marion's real estate office, the bank, and the Community Church were all on the riverside of the street and would be hardest hit. But if the waters rose as high as the weather service was predicting, both sides of Piedmont Avenue would be inundated.

"You need to evacuate. Now."

Jodie turned to find Brynn, a yellow rain slicker over her uniform, standing in the doorway to the deck.

"We've done as much here as we can," Jodie admitted.

"You'll be safe at your folks'," Brynn said. "The water won't reach that far."

Jodie shook her head. "We'll join the volunteers on the barricades."

"Be careful," Brynn warned and hurried away, apparently to issue the same evacuation advice to other merchants along the street.

By the time Jodie and Jeff had returned to Pleasant Valley earlier, many town residents had already swarmed to the riverbank to fill and stack sandbags against the rising waters. That barrier was downtown's only hope. The governor had called up the National Guard, but their mobilization took time, and the troops weren't expected to arrive for several more hours.

After returning from Columbia, Jeff had dropped Jodie off and headed for Archer Farm. Jodie had been so distracted by the imminent disaster, she'd barely spoken during the ride home. She'd wanted to savor the memories of their night together, but circumstances hadn't allowed time to think for longer than a few minutes about anything but saving her business.

Jodie suppressed an overwhelming urge to rage and shake her fists at the heavens. She'd worked seven long, hard years to build her café and shop into a business she could be proud of, and by this time tomorrow, all of it could be washed away. On top of that, her relationship with Brittany was tenuous at best, and Jodie found herself hopelessly in love with a man who admitted they had no future together. A weaker part of her wanted to curl into a ball and hide. But the better half of her nature, the strength that had seen her through a teen pregnancy, raising a child and developing a business from scratch stiffened her spine and her resolve.

"You go on to Grandma's," she told Brittany. She hadn't even had a chance yet to talk with her daughter about running away. That serious discussion and the resulting consequences for Brittany would have to wait until the flood waters receded.

"I can help with the sandbags," Brit insisted with a stubbornness that Jodie recognized as exactly like her own.

She threw her arm around her daughter's shoulders and hugged her. "You're sure?"

Brit nodded. "I'm not tired."

Jodie knew better. Neither had slept much the night

before, and they'd both worn themselves out dragging the contents of the café and shop up the stairs, but if Brittany wanted to fill sandbags, Jodie wouldn't discourage her. Waiting at the Nathan house for the river to rise would drive them both nuts.

After stopping in the hardware store to tell her folks where they were going, Jodie and Brittany followed the alley between the two buildings to the riverbank. Jodie had expected chaos, but the townspeople had organized into relay lines that ran from the river's edge back to the stacks of empty bags and piles of sand dumped by the trucks from the lumberyard. Along the bank, a protective wall of sandbags rose ever so slowly. Gauging the gradual increase of the barricade's height against the rapidly rising torrent, Jodie didn't hold out much hope of saving the town.

Among the rain gear and slickers of the townsfolk were men and boys dressed in the soaked olive-drab T-shirts and cargo shorts of Archer Farm. Even in the downpour, Jodie identified Gofer, Kermit, Trace, Ricochet and Jeff, who'd apparently coordinated the lines of volunteers with military efficiency. The teens of Archer Farms were working hard, too. The battle-hardened Marines and the physically fit teenagers filled and moved the heavy bags with ease, efficiency and amazing speed.

Hefting a wet, sand-loaded bag as easily as if it were filled with straw, Jeff passed it to Jay-Jay behind him and, in the process, caught Jodie's eye. With a nod and a soul-searing look from his storm-gray eyes, he acknowledged her briefly, then turned to take the next bag in the unending line.

Brittany slogged her way through the thick red mud into a line beside Daniel, and Jodie fell in place behind Marion Sawyer, who threw her a grim smile before manhandling the next bag and passing it on.

For the next two hours, hair plastered to her head, her sneakers oozing with mud, her body screaming with fatigue, Jodie wrestled the heavy bags from Marion and stacked them onto the wall she hoped would eventually stem the swiftly rising current. To block out her agony, she kept her eyes on Jeff, muscles straining effortlessly under his wet T-shirt, the strong line of his jaw set with determination, his steady words of encouragement sometimes penetrating the rumble of the river and the spatter of the rain.

A few feet away, Brittany worked at the end of another line. As the barrier grew taller, Brit scrambled atop the wall to take the bags Daniel hoisted up to her. With a surge of love and pride, Jodie observed her daughter slap a bag in place, swipe her hair back from her face and flash her a smile.

Maybe things between them were going to be okay, Jodie thought with a ray of hope. Nothing like adversity to draw families together.

But the next bag Daniel tossed Brittany overbalanced her, and before Jodie's horrified eyes, her daughter windmilled her arms, teetered briefly, and pitched backward into the roaring river.

"Noooo!" Jodie screamed, but the wind snatched her cry away.

Jodie scrambled onto the wall, ran atop it alongside the river until she caught up with Brittany, tossed like a piece of balsa wood on the raging current. Without a thought for her own safety, Jodie plunged in after her.

Icy, murky water closed over her head, buffeted her like the full force of a water cannon, and dragged her toward the bottom. She kicked hard and fought her way to the surface. She spotted something in the water near her, shot out her hand, and grasped the back of Brittany's shirt. Using strength she hadn't known she possessed, she pulled her daughter toward her. Brittany sputtered, choked and grabbed Jodie around the neck in a panicked move that sent them both spiraling beneath the surface again.

Her lungs screaming for air, Jodie kicked with all her strength, but Brittany's weight dragged against her own.

They were both going to drown.

MOVING WITH THE EASE and effectiveness of a well-oiled machine, Jeff lifted each filled bag and tossed it to Jay-Jay behind him. He'd started a running tally but lost it at the one-hundred-and-fifty-second bag when Jodie had appeared at the rear of the line beside him. Now, while he automatically caught each bag and heaved it down the line, his gaze sought Jodie and watched her grapple with the heavy bags without complaint and with amazing strength for a woman who weighed barely over a hundred pounds, literally soaking wet.

He turned to receive a bag from young Jason on the line in front of him, and when he handed it off to Jay-Jay, Jodie had disappeared. He searched the crowd and caught sight of her racing along the top of the barricade. When she suddenly dived into the turbulent river, his heart slammed into his throat.

Fear almost paralyzed him until his Marine training kicked in, thrust his emotions aside and made him focus on what had to be done.

He grabbed Jason and yelled in his ear above the rain and river noise. "Jodie's in the river. Tell the staff to get ropes and come help."

Before Jason could answer, Jeff hit the bank at a dead run, spattering mud. He vaulted over the wall downriver from where Jodie had disappeared, and flung himself headlong into the water.

Treading hard to keep his head above the surface, he scanned the river, but the roiling whitewater showed no sign of Jodie.

Then a flash of pale skin, the briefest flutter of a hand thrust above the rapids, appeared upriver. Knowing he couldn't swim against the current, Jeff took several strong strokes crosswise to position himself in Jodie's path.

He drew closer and saw her struggling with someone else. Seizing Jodie, who had latched onto the other person, he thanked God for the physical training that had developed the powerful muscles of his legs and enabled him to keep all of them afloat.

His confidence faltered slightly when he realized how close the relentless current shoved them toward the main bridge into town, only a hundred yards downstream and now underwater. If they tried to go beneath the bridge, they'd drown, but the water wasn't high enough to carry them over it. Unless he could get them all to the bank damned quick, they would be squashed like bugs against the bridge pilings.

To his left, Kermit, Trace, Ricochet and Gofer raced along the narrow strip of bank below the sandbag wall. Kermit flung the coiled rope he carried. Hanging on to Jodie with one hand, Jeff lunged for it with the other.

And missed.

With another powerful kick, Jeff maneuvered closer to the bank. The sweeping branches of a weeping willow arched just above the surface far out into the river. Jeff grabbed a branch and held on. Only then did he realize that the person with Jodie was Brittany. While Jodie was alert and bright-eyed, Brittany was deathly pale, eyes closed, lips blue. He couldn't tell if she was breathing.

Kermit had retrieved the rope and flung it again. This time Jeff caught it.

"Take Brittany first," Jodie screamed in his ear.

Jeff didn't argue. The kid was in bad shape and needed help fast. "Can you hang on till I get back?"

Jodie nodded and wrapped one hand around the willow branch. When Jeff grabbed Brittany from her, Jodie latched on to the willow with the other hand, too.

With the rope tied around his waist, his team, braced on the bank, hauled him in slowly while he struggled to keep Brittany's head above water. He didn't dare look back to check on Jodie for fear of being inundated and losing the teen, but he could feel Jodie's eyes locked on him, could feel her spirit urging him on.

As soon as Jeff's feet touched the bank, Gofer took Brittany from his arms.

Brynn appeared beside him. "Bring her this way. The paramedics are almost here."

Assured Brittany was in good hands, Jeff secured the rope around his waist and plunged once more into the deadly current. The water's movement took him instantly toward Jodie, who still clung to the branch, even though the water and the debris it carried battered her like a piñata.

Carried by the current, he overshot the branch, but

the team hauled on the rope until he was within reach of her. He slid his arms beneath hers and felt her body jerk away, tugged by the current as she released her stranglehold on the willow. At the same time she threw her arms around his neck and held on.

Within minutes the team had hauled them both onto the bank. Jodie slid from his grasp and glanced around, obviously frantic. "Where's Brittany?"

Brynn took her arms. "She's on her way to the hospital. I'll take you."

"I'm coming with you," Jeff said.

Jodie glanced at the steadily rising water and shook her head. "You're needed here."

He glanced at Brynn. "You coming back?"

The officer nodded. "But we'll pick up Jodie's parents on the way to the hospital. I won't leave her alone."

Jeff spoke to Brynn but kept his eyes on Jodie. "And you'll bring me a report?"

"As soon as I get back."

Jeff wanted to go with them, to make sure that Brittany was all right, to reassure Jodie, but the two women had already disappeared into the crowd of volunteers. Knowing he'd be more useful where he was, he ordered his team back into their lines and reached for the next sandbag.

JODIE PACED THE CORRIDOR of Pleasant Valley Hospital, waiting for the doctor's report. He'd ordered her from Brittany's bedside while he performed his latest examination. It had been almost two hours since Jeff had rescued her and Brittany from the river, two long hours that Brittany's life had hung in the balance and the E.R. doctors and staff had worked furiously to save her daughter. Something in the water had struck Brittany's head, causing her to lose consciousness. Although the doctor had cleared her lungs, he was waiting for her to wake up to assess the extent of any damage.

Jodie's parents sat in the hard plastic chairs of the waiting room, talking quietly. Grant and Merrilee had gone to the cafeteria for coffee. The hospital itself seemed eerily quiet. Only the occasional ring of a telephone, a call for a doctor over the intercom, and the whir of a machine at the end of the hall, polishing the highly waxed floors, broke the silence.

When the automatic doors at the entrance slid open, Jeff strode toward her. His clothes were muddy and wet, his expression grim, his hair slicked against his head from the rain, and his wet boots squished with each step.

He'd never looked more handsome, and she'd never been so glad to see anyone in her life.

She hurried toward him, and he opened his arms. For the first time since she'd watch Brittany fall into the river, Jodie felt a flicker of relief.

Jeff hugged her tight, then held her at arm's length.

His somber eyes searched her face. "Has there been any change? Brynn's latest update was the same."

Jodie's breath hitched in her throat, and she had to swallow before she spoke. "We're still waiting for the doctor's report."

"I'll wait with you."

Jodie shivered in the too-cool air-conditioning. Even though her mother had brought her dry garments, she was freezing, and Jeff had to be miserable in his wet clothes. But if he was, he didn't show it. He pulled her into a chair beside him and laced his fingers through hers.

"I haven't thanked you—"

"No need." His voice was low, intimate. "I was saving my own life. I couldn't live without you, Jodie."

Tears welled in her eyes. "And I can't live without Brittany. You saved her, too. I'll never forget that."

At the soft thud of approaching footsteps, she lifted her head. Dr. Anderson, the young new E.R. specialist, had left Brittany's room and was coming down the hall toward her.

Jodie stood. Jeff rose beside her.

"She's awake," Dr. Anderson said. "And other than a nasty headache, she seems fine."

"Thank God." Jodie's legs threatened to give way. Only Jeff's strong arm kept her upright.

"We'll keep her overnight for observation," Dr. Anderson said, "but it's just a precaution."

Jodie's parents, Grant and Merrilee joined them and heard the news. Their praise for Jeff's rescue was effusive, and Jodie could tell he was uncomfortable from the attention.

Brynn's sudden arrival interrupted their celebration, and cold dread gripped Jodie once more.

She'd forgotten about the river.

Chapter Thirteen

Jodie turned her van onto the road leading to Archer Farm. Butterflies dived like kamikaze fighters in her stomach, and her palms were damp with nervous perspiration. Jeff, whom she hadn't seen since that evening in the hospital corridor, had called and asked her to come to Archer Farm. He'd refused to say more, insisting he'd explain when she arrived.

He'd sent Brittany get-well flowers and a stuffed animal—a uniformed bulldog, the Marine Corps mascot. But today was the first time Jodie had spoken with him since the flood a week ago. Jeff had slipped away in the excitement over Dr. Anderson's news of Brittany's imminent recovery and, according to Brynn, returned to the riverbank.

Thanks to National Guard reinforcements and an unexpected fast-moving front that pushed the rains through the area more swiftly than expected, the river hadn't risen as high as predicted. The wall of sandbags had protected the town. Only an outbuilding at

the Community Church that stored newspapers for re-
cycling had suffered any damage.

Jeff, his staff, and the boys from Archer Farm had
been declared heroes by the local paper. Agnes Tuttle's petitions had been destroyed at the request of
those who'd signed them, and Jeff's entire group
would be honored at the town's Fourth of July celebration in a few days.

Jodie eased the van up the final ascent to the farm.
She'd had an entire week to return to normal, but her
life would never be normal again. She couldn't get
Jeff out of her mind. Or her heart. He'd risked his
life for her and Brittany.

And before that, he'd made love to Jodie with a
passion and tenderness she'd never imagined possible. But this past week was a testament to the sepa-
rateness of their lives. Jodie had worked long hours
to put her café and shop back in order after the hasty
evacuation, and she'd worked even harder to establish
a dialogue with Brittany. She didn't know how Jeff
had spent his week, but he'd obviously had no time
for Jodie.

So why did he want to see her now?

She parked in front of the farmhouse. Jeff, who'd
been waiting on the porch, came to meet her as she
climbed out of the van. Today, instead of the olive-
drab uniform of Archer Farm, he wore black slacks
and a gray knit shirt the color of his eyes. His expression gave no hint of his thoughts.

"Thanks for coming," he said.

She glanced around and noted, except for Jeff's pickup, no other vehicles or people in sight. "Where is everybody?"

"Field trip to the Blue Ridge Parkway."

"You didn't go?"

"I have more important things to take care of."

"Then you'd better tell me what you wanted, so I can leave you to them."

Her nervousness increased at the realization they were alone. She remembered all too well what had happened the last time, and although she'd treasure that memory the rest of her life, she refused to indulge in sex again without commitment.

"How's Brittany?" he asked.

"Physically she's fine. But emotionally she still has issues."

"Still angry with you?"

Jodie shook her head. "After I jumped in the river after her, she can't refute how much I love her. It's her paternal grandparents' lack of acknowledgment that still hurts."

"And you?"

"What about me?"

"How are you?"

"Fine."

"Oh." He sounded disappointed.

"Why shouldn't I be?" she said, her defenses up.

"No reason. It's good you're okay." But he didn't sound convinced.

"Why am I here?" she asked.

"Because I'm not okay."

Alarm cascaded through her. "What's wrong?"

He shrugged. "Can't eat. Can't sleep. Can't concentrate."

She studied him closely. To her eyes he'd never looked better. "Have you seen a doctor?"

He nodded solemnly. "Dr. Hager."

She took a moment to make the connection. "Gofer?"

"He has his Ph.D. in psychology, remember?"

"And did Dr. Hager make a diagnosis?"

Jeff took her hand and led her to a rocker on the porch. She took a seat, and he propped a hip on the balustrade across from her.

After a long pause during which his eyes never left hers, he spoke. "Gofer says there's only one cure for what ails me."

Sex, Jodie thought, but she wasn't going there again, no matter how much she wanted him.

"Marry me," Jeff said, shattering her thoughts.

"What?" She couldn't believe she'd heard him correctly. They'd both agreed there was no room for marriage in either of their lives. They each had too many other commitments.

"I know Brittany may have problems with us," Jeff was saying, "but I have the name of a marriage and family therapist in Greenville who's top-notch. The three of us can go together. I'll do whatever it takes to help Brittany accept that you deserve a life of your own.''

''But what about Archer Farm?''

''The story of our boys' help during the flood hit the national papers. As a result, funding has been pouring into the project. With proper investment, we have enough to keep us in business for years and pay decent salaries to the staff. My job's been made a whole lot easier, giving me time to devote to you, to us.''

Events were moving too fast. Her heart was pounding, her head spinning, her stomach clenching. For one terrified moment she feared she'd be sick from excitement right on Jeff's front porch. She forced herself to breathe.

''But where would we live?'' She thought of her business. And Jeff was needed at the farm.

''We don't have to decide now,'' he said with a calmness she envied, considering the way her entire body was in chaos. ''We don't even have to be married right away. If the therapist thinks it's best, we can wait till Brittany goes away to college.''

''That long?'' Jodie's voice rose in protest.

''I take it that's a *yes?*''

''What?'' Her thoughts whirled, and she was having trouble breathing.

He reached for her and drew her into his arms. "Will you marry me, Jodie Nathan?"

"Oh, yes, but—"

"We'll take care of the *buts* later. For now, just shut up and kiss me."

And she did.

Epilogue

Spring in the valley was Jodie's favorite time of year. March had come in like a lamb with sunny skies, balmy temperatures and a profusion of forsythia, daffodils and the bridal-white blossoms of Bradford pear trees.

Spring had also brought the apple blossoms and paper whites that filled Jodie's bouquet, the one she'd be tossing at the reception in a few minutes, as soon as she shed her wedding gown for traveling clothes.

Jeff stood behind her in the large master bedroom of the house at Archer Farm and wrapped his arms around her waist. She gazed at their reflection in the tall mirror on the dresser and thought for the thousandth time how amazingly handsome he looked in his tuxedo. But she wasn't surprised. Jeff was gorgeous in anything. Or nothing.

Jodie resisted the urge to pinch herself to see if she was dreaming. She still couldn't believe her good fortune, being loved by a man both intrinsically good and sinfully good-looking.

"You okay?" he asked.

"Just dazed." She leaned against him. "I can't believe we're really married."

The ceremony at the Community Church and the reception at the farm had passed in a blur, unlike the previous eight months, which had seemed to last forever. But that time had been well spent. She and Brittany or sometimes Jodie and Jeff and often all three of them had spent weekly sessions with the marriage and family therapist in Greenville.

As first, the mere idea of loving Jeff, let alone marriage, had scared Jodie to death. She'd messed up her young life so badly with Randy Mercer, the prospect of a real relationship practically paralyzed her. But with the counselor's guidance and Jeff's gentle support and unshakable love, her fears had gradually disappeared. Not that Jodie felt she wouldn't make some mistakes, but she'd learned she could handle them if she did.

Together, Jodie, Jeff and Brittany had worked out most of their issues.

Such as where they'd live. After much discussion and compromise, the three had agreed that Jodie and Brittany would move into the house at Archer Farm after the honeymoon. By renting the apartment over her café, Jodie could afford to hire a manager for the business, freeing time to spend with Brittany and also to provide a maternal presence for the Archer Farm boys.

The therapist had helped Brittany deal with her anger over her father and grandparents' desertion, anger that she'd transferred to Jodie. Brittany had also accepted that her mother's love for Jeff didn't take away from Jodie's love for her. And Brittany was growing fond of Jeff, too. The only thing the therapist hadn't resolved was the fact that Brit was still a teenager. Only time, Jodie thought with a smile, would cure that affliction. Meanwhile, their future as a family looked promising.

"We're married all right," Jeff assured her with a grin. "And between Trace and Grant, we have several hours of video footage to prove it."

"Don't forget Merrilee's photographs." Jodie brushed a fleck of icing from his lapel. "I've never cut a cake with a sword before."

"Just another Marine tradition." The devotion in his warm gray eyes reinforced her conviction that marrying Jeff was the best decision she'd ever made.

"Something tells me there're lots of Marine traditions in my future."

"Is that a problem?"

She leaned her cheek against his chest. "I married a Marine, traditions and all."

His arms tightened around her, and she'd never felt more cherished, more secure. "And this Marine is going to love you always," he promised.

"Always?"

"Forever and ever, amen," Jeff echoed the Randy Travis song that had played at the reception, still going strong in the great room next door.

She lifted her face to his, eyes shining. "Forever is a long time."

"For loving you, Jodie Nathan Davidson, forever isn't long enough."

* * * * *

Look for the next book in
Charlotte Douglas's new miniseries,
A PLACE TO CALL HOME,
SPRING IN THE VALLEY,
coming in April 2005.

Turn the page for excerpts from next month's four lively and delightful books from American Romance!

Archer's Angels by Tina Leonard (#1053)
Archer Jefferson—he's brother number eight in Tina's COWBOYS BY THE DOZEN miniseries. Enjoy this popular author's high-energy writing, quirky characters and outrageous situations. Come back for more with Belonging to Bandera! Available in February 2005.

Clove Penmire looked around as she got off the bus in Lonely Hearts Station, Texas. For all her fascination with cowboys and the lure of the dusty state she'd read so much about, she had to admit that small-town Texas was nothing like her homeland of Australia.

A horse broke free from the barn across the street, walking itself nonchalantly between the two sides of the old-time town. A cowboy sprinted out of the barn and ran after his horse, but he was laughing as he caught up to it.

Clove smiled. From the back she couldn't tell if the man was handsome, but he was dressed in Wranglers and a hat, and as far as she could tell, this cowboy was the real thing.

And she had traveled to Texas for the real thing.

That sentiment would have sounded preposterous, even to Clove, just a month ago. Until she'd learned that her sister, Lucy, couldn't have a baby. Of course, people all over the world couldn't always conceive when they wanted to. They adopted, or pursued other means of happiness. She hadn't been too worried-until Lucy had confessed that she thought her husband might leave her for a woman who could bear children.

Clove's thoughts then took a decidedly new trajectory, one that included fantasies of tossing her brother-in-law into the ocean.

Now the cowboy caught her interested gaze, holding it for just a second before he looked back at his horse. The man was extremely handsome. Breathtakingly so. Not the cowboy for her, considering her mission, and the fact that she was what people politely referred to as…a girl with a good personality.

She sighed. If Lucy had gotten all the beauty, their mother always said with a gentle smile, then Clove had gotten all the bravery. Which was likely how she'd ended up as a stuntwoman.

She watched the cowboy brush his horse's back with one hand, and fan a fly away from its lovely flame-marked face. He was still talking to it; she could hear low murmuring that sounded very sexy, especially since she'd never heard a man murmur in a husky voice to her.

"Archer Jefferson!" someone yelled from inside the barn. "Get that cotton-pickin', apple-stealin', dog-faced Appaloosa in here!"

"Insult the man, but not the sexy beast!" he yelled back.

Clove gasped. Archer Jefferson! The man she'd traveled several time zones to see! Her TexasArcher of two years' worth of e-mail correspondence!

He was all cowboy, more cowboy than she'd come mentally prepared to corral. "Whoa," she murmured to herself.

Okay, a man that drool-worthy did not lack female friends. Why had he spent two years writing to a woman he'd never meet? She wrinkled her nose, pushed her thick glasses up on her nose and studied him further. Tight jeans, dirty boots. Long, black hair under a black felt hat—he'd never mentioned long hair in their correspondence. Deep voice. Piercing blue eyes, she noted as he turned around, catching her still staring at him. She jumped, he laughed and then he tipped his hat to her as he swung up onto the "dog-faced" Appaloosa, riding it into the barn in a manner the stuntwoman in her appreciated.

Just how difficult would it be to entice that cowboy into her bed? Archer had put ideas about his virility in her mind, with his Texas-sized bragging about his manliness and the babies popping out all over Malfunction Junction ranch.

Seeing him, however, made her think that perhaps he hadn't been bragging as much as stating fact. Her heart beat faster. He'd said he wasn't in the relationship market.

But a baby, just one baby....

Her Secret Valentine by Cathy Gillen Thacker (#1054)
This is the entertaining and emotional fifth installment
in Cathy's series, THE BRIDES OF HOLLY
SPRINGS. With a little help from Cupid—and the
close-knit Hart clan—a long-distance couple has a
Valentine's Day reunion they'll never forget! You'll
be captivated by Cathy's trademark charm, but you'll
also identify with the real issues explored in this
book—the tough choices faced by a two-career couple in today's world. Available in February 2005.

"How long is this situation between you and Ashley
going to go on?" Mac Hart asked.

Cal tensed. He thought he'd been invited over to
his brother Mac's house to watch playoff football
with the rest of the men in the family. Now, suddenly,
it was looking more like an intervention. He leaned
forward to help himself to some of the nachos on the

coffee table in front of the sofa. "I don't know what you mean."

"Then let us spell it out for you," Cal's brother-in-law, Thad Lantz, said with his usual coachlike efficiency.

Joe continued. "She missed Janey's wedding to Thad in August, as well as Fletcher's marriage to Lily in October, and Dylan and Hannah's wedding in November."

Cal bristled. They all knew Ashley was busy completing her OB/GYN fellowship in Honolulu. "She wanted to be here but since the flight from Honolulu to Raleigh is at least twelve hours, it's too far to go for a weekend trip. Not that she has many full weekends off in any case." Nor did he. Hence, their habit of rendezvousing in San Francisco, since it was a six- or seven-hour flight for each of them.

More skeptical looks. "She didn't make it back to Carolina for Thanksgiving or Christmas or New Year's this year, either," Dylan observed.

Cal shrugged and centered his attention on the TV, where a log of pregame nonsense was taking place. "She had to work all three holidays." He wished the game would hurry up and start. Because the sooner it did, the sooner this conversation would be over.

"'Had to,' or volunteered?" Fletcher murmured with a questioning lift of his dark eyebrows.

Uneasiness settled on Cal. He'd had many of the same questions himself. Still, Ashley was his wife, and he felt honor-bound to defend her. "I saw her in November in San Francisco. We celebrated all our holidays then." In one passion-filled weekend that had, oddly enough, left him feeling lonelier and more uncertain of their union than ever.

Concerned looks were exchanged all around. Cal knew the guys in the family all felt sorry for him, which just made the situation worse.

Dylan dipped a tortilla chip into the chili-cheese sauce. "So when's Ashley coming home?" he asked curiously.

That was just it—Cal didn't know. Ashley didn't want to talk about it. "Soon," he fibbed.

All eyes turned to him. Cal waited expectantly, knowing from the silence that there was more. Finally, Joe cleared his throat. "The women in the family are all upset. You've been married nearly three years now, and most of that time you and Ashley have been living apart."

"So?" Cal prodded.

"So, they're tired of seeing you unhappy." Dylan took over where Cal had left off. "They're giving you and Ashley till Valentine's Day—"

Their wedding anniversary.

"—to make things right."

"And if that doesn't happen?" Cal demanded.

Fletcher scowled. "Then the women in the family are stepping in."

Cupid and the Cowboy by Carol Finch (#1055)
Carol Finch is a widely published author making her debut in American Romance—and we're delighted to welcome her! She writes with genuine wit and charm, and she brings you characters you'll like instantly—not to mention a wonderful and vivid sense of place. You'll soon discover that Moon Valley, Texas, is your kind of town.... Available in February 2005.

"Damn, here she comes again."

Third time this week that Erika Dunn had shown up uninvited at his ranch house. She was making it difficult for Judd to settle into his self-imposed role as a recluse.

Judd Foster peered through the dusty slats of the miniblinds and heavy, outdated drapes that covered his living room window. She had the kind of unadvertised and understated beauty that intrigued a man who'd been trained to look beyond surface appearances. The woman didn't just walk to his house; she practically floated. She was too vibrant, too energized. He didn't want her coming around, spreading good cheer and flashing that infectious smile.

He just wanted to be left alone.

His attention shifted to the covered dish in her hand. Judd's mouth watered involuntarily. He wondered what delicious culinary temptation she had delivered this time. More of that melt-in-your-mouth smoked chicken that had been marinated in pineapple juice and coated with her secret concoction of herbs and spices? Or something equally delectable? Apparently, Erika figured the most effective way to coax a man out of his property was to sabotage his taste buds and his stomach.

Judd focused on Erika's face. Her face was wholesome and animated and her eyes reminded him of a cloudless sky. Her ivory skin, dotted with freckles on her upturned nose, made her look fragile and delicate—a blatant contrast to her assertive, bubbly personality. She was part bombshell-in-hiding and part girl-next-door. A woman of interesting contrasts and potential.

Judd watched Erika balance the covered plate in one hand while she hammered on the front door with the other. He knew she wouldn't give up and go away, so he opened the door before she pounded a hole in it. "Now what?" he demanded.

Erika beamed an enthusiastic greeting as she sailed, uninvited, into his house.

The instant Judd felt himself leaning impulsively toward her, he withdrew and stiffened his resistance. "The answer is still no," he said right off.

Might as well beat her to the punch and hope she'd give up her ongoing crusade to buy his property. He didn't want her to sweet-talk him into signing over the old barn that held fond childhood memories. He didn't want to salivate like Pavlov's dogs when the aromatic smoked meat, piled beneath a layer of aluminum foil, whetted his appetite.

Undaunted, Erika thrust the heaping plate at him and smiled radiantly. "No what? No, you won't do me a favor by taking this extra food off my hands? No, you've decided to stop eating altogether?"

She glanced around the gloomy living room, shook her head in disapproval, then strode to the west window. "Really, Judd, it should be a criminal offense to keep this grand old house enshrouded in darkness. It looks like vampire headquarters."

Leaving him holding the plate, she threw open the drapes, jerked up the blinds and opened all three living room windows. Fresh air poured into the room, carrying her scent to him. Judd winced when blinding sunbeams speared into the room, spotlighting Erika's alluring profile—as if he needed another reminder of how well proportioned she was.

He didn't. Furthermore, he didn't want to deal with the lusty thoughts her appearance provoked. He didn't want to like anything about Erika Dunn. Erika was too attractive, too optimistic. Too everything for a man who'd become cynical and world-weary after years of belly-crawling around hellholes in Third World countries.

He wondered what it was going to take to discourage Erika from waltzing in here as if she owned the place and trying to befriend a man who was completely unworthy of friendship. He hadn't been able to protect the one true friend he'd had in the past decade and that tormented him. He didn't want anyone to depend on him or expect anything from him.

Emergency Engagement by Michele Dunaway (#1056)
In this emotional story by Michele Dunaway, you'll
find a classic plot—the "engagement of convenience"—and a group of very contemporary characters. Michele is known for this appealing combination
of enduring themes and likable characters who live
up-to-the-minute lives! Available in February 2005.

He wasn't supposed to be there. It wasn't his night;
in fact, this week he wasn't supposed to deal with any
emergencies unless they occurred during normal office hours.

But because of a wedding, there'd been a shortage
of pediatricians to staff the pediatric emergency floor.
So, when his partner had asked, Quinton had agreed
to take Bart's shift. Even though it was a Friday night,
Quinton had nothing better to do.

Which, when he stopped to think about it, was pathetic. He, Dr. Quinton Searle, pediatric specialist,

should have something to do. At thirty-five, he should have some woman to date, some place to be, something.

But the truth was that he didn't, which was why, when the call came through, he was in the wrong place at the right time. He turned to Elaine. He liked working with her. At fifty-something she'd seen it all, and was a model of brisk efficiency, the most reliable nurse in any crisis. "What have I got?" he asked.

"Four-year-old child. Poison Control just called. The kid ate the mother's cold medicine. Thought it was green candy."

He frowned as he contemplated the situation. "How many?"

Elaine checked her notes. "The mother thinks it was only two tablets, but she isn't sure. The container's empty."

Great, Quinton thought. He hated variables. "Is she here yet?"

Elaine shook her head. "Any minute. She's on her way. Downstairs knows to buzz me immediately so we can bring the kid right up."

Quinton nodded. "Downstairs" was slang for the main emergency room. As part of the Chicago Presbyterian Hospital's patient care plan, a separate emergency floor had been set up especially for children. Children were triaged in the main E.R., and then sent up to the pediatric E.R. He shoved his hand into the pocket of his white doctor's coat. "Let me know the minute you get the buzz."

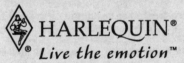

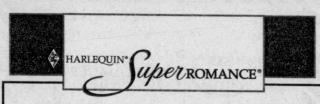

A six-book series from Harlequin Superromance

WOMEN *in Blue*

Six female cops battling crime and corruption on the streets of Houston. Together they can fight the blue wall of silence. But divided, will they fall?

Coming in February 2005, *She Walks the Line* by Roz Denny Fox (Harlequin Superromance #1254)

As a Chinese woman in the Houston Police Department, Mei Lu Ling is a minority twice over. She once worked for her father, a renowned art dealer specializing in Asian artifacts, so her new assignment—tracking art stolen from Chinese museums—is a logical one. But when she's required to work with Cullen Archer, an insurance investigator connected to Interpol, her reaction is more emotional than logical. Because she could easily fall in love with this man…and his adorable twins.

Coming in March 2005, *A Mother's Vow* by K. N. Casper (Harlequin Superromance #1260)

There is corruption in Police Chief Catherine Tanner's department. So when evidence turns up to indicate that her husband may not have died of natural causes, she has to go outside her own precinct to investigate. Ex-cop Jeff Rowan is the most logical person for her to turn to. Unfortunately, Jeff isn't inclined to help Catherine, considering she was the one who fired him.

Available wherever Harlequin books are sold.

Also in the series:
The Partner by Kay David (#1230, October 2004)
The Children's Cop by Sherry Lewis (#1237, November 2004)
The Witness by Linda Style (#1243, December 2004)
Her Little Secret by Anna Adams (#1248, January 2005)

If you enjoyed what you just read,
then we've got an offer you can't resist!

Take 2 bestselling
love stories FREE!
Plus get a FREE surprise gift!

The world's bestselling romance series.

HARLEQUIN®
Presents
Seduction and Passion Guaranteed!

GREEK TYCOONS

They're the men who have everything—except a bride....

Wealth, power, charm—what else could a heart-stoppingly
handsome tycoon need? In the GREEK TYCOONS
miniseries you have already been introduced to some
gorgeous Greek multimillionaires who are in need of wives.

THE GREEK BOSS'S DEMAND
by *Trish Morey*
On sale January 2005, #2444

THE GREEK TYCOON'S
CONVENIENT MISTRESS
by *Lynne Graham*
On sale February 2005, #2445

THE GREEK'S
SEVEN-DAY SEDUCTION
by *Susan Stephens*
On sale March 2005, #2455

Pick up a Harlequin Presents® novel and you will enter a world
of spine-tingling passion and provocative, tantalizing romance!

Available wherever Harlequin books are sold.

www.eHarlequin.com   HPTGTY0105

The world's bestselling romance series.

The world's bestselling romance series.

HARLEQUIN®
Presents

Seduction and Passion Guaranteed!

Back by popular demand...

EXPECTING!

She's sexy, successful and **PREGNANT!**

Relax and enjoy our fabulous series about couples whose passion results in pregnancies... sometimes unexpected!

Share the surprises, emotions, drama and suspense as our parents-to-be come to terms with the prospect of bringing a new life into the world. All will discover that the business of making babies brings with it the most special love of all....

Our next arrival will be

HIS PREGNANCY BARGAIN by *Kim Lawrence*
On sale January 2005, #2441
Don't miss it!

THE BRABANTI BABY by *Catherine Spencer*
On sale February 2005, #2450

Lost & Found

Somebody's Daughter
by Rebecca Winters
Harlequin Superromance #1259

Twenty-six years ago, baby Kathryn was taken from the McFarland family. Now Kit Burke has discovered that she might have been that baby. Will her efforts to track down her real family lead Kit into their loving arms? Or will discovering that she is a McFarland mean disaster for her and the man she loves?

Available February 2005 wherever Harlequin books are sold.

Remember to look for these Rebecca Winters titles, available from Harlequin Romance:

To Catch a Groom (Harlequin Romance #3819)—on sale November 2004
To Win His Heart (Harlequin Romance #3827)—on sale January 2005
To Marry for Duty (Harlequin Romance #3835)—on sale March 2005

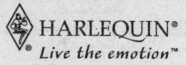

HARLEQUIN®
Live the emotion™